VEGAS,
Baby

THEODORA TAYLOR

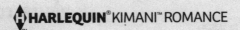

HARLEQUIN® KIMANI™ ROMANCE

To my lovely one-click readers.
I hope you love this story.

Recycling programs
for this product may
not exist in your area.

ISBN-13: 978-0-373-86380-8

Vegas, Baby

Copyright © 2014 by Ernessa Carter

For questions and comments about the quality of this book please contact us
at CustomerService@Harlequin.com.

(H) HARLEQUIN®
™ www.Harlequin.com

Printed in U.S.A.

Dear Reader,

I loved the remake of *Ocean's Eleven* and found the main antagonist, Terry Benedict, fascinating. I'm a writer who tends to be more interested in the villains than the heroes while watching movies, so he sent my mind into full spin. I hope you enjoy this tale about an ambitious, uptight businessman who gets thrown for a love loop by a sassy showgirl. Sunny and Cole are a smoking-hot couple, and their story sizzles like the Vegas summer.

My very best,

Theodora

Chapter 1

"You want me to do *what?*"

Cole Benton didn't shout, but he didn't have to. His voice carried enough icicles to let the woman sitting in his black guest chair know he was beyond not pleased. It was the same tone he used with employees both on and below the executive floor when they were dangerously close to getting fired.

But his grandmother, Nora Benton, or as she liked to refer to herself, "the best damn showgirl this town has ever seen," just crossed her long legs. She liked to show them off—to the point that she ordered her Chanel suits with a higher hemline than was normally deemed appropriate for her age set.

"You heard me, luv," she answered, her Irish accent reinforcing her words with steely determination. "I'm telling you, it's for your own good."

"And I'm telling you, you need an MRI if you think I'm going to marry some showgirl…"

"Sunny's not just *some* showgirl," Nora said, patting her mane of wavy hair, which thanks to her twice monthly hair appointments, was still as glossy and vibrant red as it had been when she and his grandfather met. "She's the granddaughter of Berta Johnson, my best friend in the entire world."

Cole gave her a skeptical look. "Your best friend whom I've never met."

"Only because she died quite a few years ago, when you were still in business school. If you'd have come to any of my last few Christmas events, you would have seen the show Sunny choreographs for herself and a few of the other Benton Girls every year. Then I would have been able to properly introduce you to Berta's lovely granddaughter."

Cole tented his hands on his desk. "Her lovely granddaughter, the showgirl."

"What's wrong with showgirls? Your grandda— God rest his soul—always said meeting me was the best thing that ever happened to him."

A shimmer of affection for the original Coleridge Benton, a stodgy businessman who'd somehow ended up married to an Irish showgirl from The Benton Hotel's revue show, made a brief pass through Cole. If not for his grandfather, he wouldn't be where he was today, the Chief Executive Officer of The Benton Group, one of the youngest CEOs of any hotel chain in Vegas history. But irritation at his grandmother soon overtook Cole's fond memory of his grandfather. Naming her chairman of The Benton Group's board before his death, so that Cole was forced to take her seriously, despite the fact that she had nothing to do with the company's day to day operations, was one of the worst business decisions his grandfather had ever made.

"With all due respect to my grandfather, he was the head of one hotel when he met you. One. I oversee a nationwide collection of The Benton Group's hotel and casino interests."

Nora's gave him a withering look. "I see, you think being a billionaire makes you too good for a showgirl then? That's what you're trying to tell the best damn showgirl this town has ever seen?"

"No, growing The Benton Group into a force to be reckoned with means I don't have time to date this girl you're trying to set me up with *or* for this inane meeting—which by the way is not remotely urgent. You told my assistant this was important."

"It is important, luv," his grandmother insisted. "I'm not getting any younger, and I'm ready for grandchildren. And with that playboy brother of yours flitting about all over Europe…"

"You should just be grateful your other grandson is running the company so well and leave it at that," he finished for her.

"Well, I've decided to take matters into my own hands," Nora said. "All you do is work, work, work." She let out an exasperated sound, as though his work was a character flaw, as opposed to what kept her in luxury cruises and Botox treatments. "Quite frankly you need to get laid well and regularly, dearie. It would do you a world of good, just like it did your grandda. It's time for you to have some fun—but only for three months, then you can settle down and give me some grandchildren."

"You want me to marry a girl I've never even met after three months of dating?" Cole asked, both his face and tone incredulous.

"Three months is generous," Nora informed him. "It only took your grandda three weeks to propose to me!"

Cole stared at his grandmother for a few long, disbelieving seconds before saying, "I have a two o'clock, so I'm calling this 'urgent meeting' to an end. Thanks for stopping by, Nora. Let's never do this again."

Nora let out a dramatic sigh. "I was afraid you might say that. I swear, the worst decision I ever made was letting your grandda take you under his wing after you got kicked out of boarding school. You've got too much of him in you and your brother has too much of me."

Cole had already turned back to his computer and started typing in notes for his two o'clock with The Benton Group's L.A. office. He was fully prepared to ignore Nora out of his office.

But then his grandmother said, "...and that's why I'll be handing over my shares in the company to your brother. I plan to make my announcement at the end of summer board meeting."

Cole's head shot up from the computer screen. His brother, Max, was the "brand ambassador" for The Benton Group. This basically meant he received a steady paycheck, which he spent on partying all over Europe. Which in turn meant his picture was regularly spread across the tabloids. It put The Benton Group in a negative light and the only reason Cole hadn't cut him off was because he had enough shares in the company to make it difficult if he decided to sell them to an outside interest. However, if Nora gave her shares to Max, then...

"That would give Max controlling interest in The Benton Group. Why would you do that?" he asked his grandmother.

Nora shrugged prettily. "Well, unlike you, luv, he came to my Christmas charity dinner and he gave Sunny and her girls some very nice compliments on their show."

"I bet," Cole said with a derisive snort. His brother wasn't the sort to miss an opportunity to flirt with scantily clad showgirls.

Nora went on, anyway. "He and I had a nice long talk the last time he was in town, and he explained to me that he'd be more than happy to stay on in Vegas and work at The Benton Group—if you weren't in charge."

Cole turned all the way around to face his grandmother. "That's never going to happen. I'm the one who built this company into a nationwide outfit. I'll be in charge of it until the day I die."

"Yes, well..." Nora played with the short hemline of her skirt. "I do miss Max, and he's promised that if I give him my shares, he'll not only marry Sunny, but give me as many grandchildren as I want."

Cole found himself once again staring at his grandmother in disbelief. "Do you have any idea of how crazy that sounds, Nora?"

Nora threw a dramatic hand across her forehead. "I do! I know it sounds crazy, luv. And of course, I'd rather Sunny marry you. You're more the settling down type—unlike Max. But I'm just so desperate for grandchildren!"

Cole would never let a business rival see him blink, and he kept his face blank as he informed Nora, "You have grandchildren. Max and I are your grandchildren."

"Hardly. Max, came out of the womb, a full blown flirt, and your derelict parents forced me to raise you, and—well, you know how difficult that was. I want a real baby, one who coos and giggles and calls me 'Gran'—not 'Nora,' like I'm one of his employees."

If Cole had a sense of humor, he might have found his grandmother's antics funny, but he didn't, especially when it came to money. "Nora, selling a controlling interest in the company I've been spent my entire career growing is not the way to get what you want."

"Don't you try to lecture me, Cole Benton. I'm not one of your underlings," his grandmother responded. "Now you either do as I say and propose to Sunny Johnson by the end of summer, or I'm selling my shares to Max!"

Nora punctuated her threat with a slap of her hand on his desk. But then her face softened. "I know what I'm threatening sounds crazy and a bit harsh, Cole. But this…" She gestured around his highrise office. "All this work and no play. It's not good for you, luv. It's made you hard. Too hard. You need something other than this business in your life."

What Nora didn't seem to understand was that this business was his life, the only thing that made his heart beat faster, the only thing that had ever given him a true return on his investment.

And he wouldn't abide anyone—even his own grandmother—threatening to compromise all the work he'd put into it.

"I've got to prepare for my two o'clock now. I'll take your request under advisement."

Nora jutted her chin into the air. "Max is coming in for the Businessman of the Year dinner on Sunday. Should I let him know he should stick around this time, and prepare to take his place as chairman of our board?"

Cole resumed typing. His grandmother may have had his grandfather wrapped around her thin finger, but Cole refused to take her bait.

And Nora seemed to understand that she was being dismissed.

She went to the door and put her hand on its chrome latch. "Understand, I'm not doing to this to hurt you or The Benton Group. I'm doing this because I care about you more than I care about this company."

Whatever it takes for her to sleep at night, Cole thought with bitter resentment. But he refused to let Nora see that she'd actually upset him. He did as he always did, focused on his work.

After Nora left, Cole finished putting in his notes for his two o'clock meeting. But as soon as he hit the last keystroke, he picked up the phone to talk to his assistant, Agnes.

"Yes, Mr. Benton," Agnes said when he buzzed her office line.

"Put in a call to Taylor Stratherford."

"Junior or Senior, sir?" she asked. Taylor Stratherford Jr. was Cole's personal lawyer, just as Stratherford Sr. had served as his grandfather's personal lawyer. However, it was Taylor Sr., who also now served as the Non-Executive Director of The Benton Group's board.

"Senior. Set up an in-person at his office as soon as

possible. Actually I want to set up one-on-ones with every member of the board except my grandmother and brother."

"Right away, Mr. Benton," Agnes answered. She was too professional to outright ask why he was asking for these meetings, but he could hear the curiosity in her voice when she asked, "Anything else?"

Cole thought about it. "Yes, get the manager of *The Benton Girls Revue* on the line, and inform him of the following..."

Chapter 2

Sunny came rushing into the backstage area of The Nora Benton Theater, still dressed in the yoga pants and tank top she'd worn to bed. And still chilled by what had happened less than thirty minutes ago back at her apartment.

She'd been so exhausted when she got home from her cocktail waitress shift on The Benton's casino floor that she'd fallen asleep on the couch while eating a meal replacement bar. She lived alone—or so she thought. That morning, she'd discovered she had a roommate, when she woke up to the sound of the alarm on her phone going off and the feel of something pulling on her hand. She'd opened her eyes to find a rat staring back at her, its beady black eyes filled with determination as its mouth tugged on the bar in her hand.

Sunny let him have it, letting the bar go with a

scream. And an hour later, she could still see the ridges on its long tail as it ran away with its treasure. She'd never be able to unsee it, and she had no idea how she was going to manage to get to sleep when she returned to her apartment after today's rehearsal, knowing that it was still there, probably lurking somewhere inside one of her walls.

With a shudder, Sunny brought her thoughts back to her present situation. How to get to the backstage dressing room without being seen by Rick.

It was exactly eleven a.m., which was their call time for their monthly rehearsal in full makeup and costumes. But Rick Rizzo was old school. Being exactly on time was the equivalent of being late in his book. He wanted all his dancers backstage at least fifteen minutes early, and if he saw her skulking through the shadows, she'd likely hear about it.

She also didn't want him to see the dark circles under her eyes. She'd never quite gotten around to telling the *Benton Girls* manager that she'd taken a second job as a cocktail waitress in the main casino. Technically, it was none of his business, but Rick was half stage dad, half control freak, and the show paid pretty well by Vegas standards with a salary, 401(K) and vacation benefits. If he saw how tired she looked without tons of concealer slathered underneath her eyes, he'd badger her until she confessed that she was planning to leave the show in late August in order to attend graduate school at New York Arts University.

They'd given her a generous scholarship, but it wasn't enough to cover any of the extras, like food and books, or rent, which was no joke. The school was located in Manhattan and didn't provide housing for grad students, but even a place in the outer boroughs of New York would set her back. So her plan was to work two jobs and save as much money as she could over the next three months.

But there was no need to tell Rick any of that yet. She knew how he'd respond: *What! You're leaving us? I gave you your first job. Bobby and I had you over for Thanksgiving Dinner every year after your grandma died, and this is how you repay me?*

Sunny knew Rick had come to count on her, not only as one of his best dancers, but also as his "work wife"—a combination of gossip buddy, friend and backstage administrator whenever Rick went on vacation. And she knew he deserved better than her just handing him a two-week notice out of the blue, but she hadn't worked up the courage to tell him.

Luckily, he was on the phone as she snuck past him backstage, telling whoever was on the other side of the line off good.

"How could you do this to me? Do you know who I am? Rick Rizzo! I made *The Benton Girls Revue*. And you think you can screw me over like this? I don't think so!"

Sunny rushed toward the dressing room, happy she'd escaped Rick's notice, but sorry for whoever was on the other side of that phone.

"Ooh, twin, you're lucky Rick didn't see you!" her friend Prudence said when Sunny dropped into her usual seat in the long line of makeup mirrors, after changing into her *Benton Girls* costume. Sunny's and Pru's costumes weren't topless, but they didn't leave much to the imagination, either, basically string bikinis, dripping in fake jewels. However, they did match, and since she and Pru were the only two black Benton Girls, with similar builds and the same big bouncy curl extensions, they often called each other "twin" when they were in costume.

"I know, right!" Sunny answered, slathering concealer onto the dark circles under her eyes. "The only reason I got away with it was because he was already yelling at somebody else on the phone when I walked in. I'm guessing it's one of the newer dancers."

The poor girl had probably called Rick to bow out of rehearsal, not realizing that Rick morphed from a loving dance dad into your worst tyrant nightmare when you broke one of his rules—like not skipping out on rehearsal without at least forty-eight hours' notice and/or a doctor's note for a fatal disease.

"Poor thing. But they've got to learn some way. I know we did." Pru said. She nudged Sunny with her elbow. "One more thing you're not going to miss about this place when you're gone, right?"

Sunny gave her friend a grateful smile. Pru was one of the few people she'd told about her plan to study dance pedagogy at New York Arts University, and she'd been nothing but supportive. They'd both started out in the chorus line at the age of twenty-two, and were both now twenty-seven. A half decade was a long time to shake your can-can for tourists, many of which were only there to see the topless girls. Pru didn't blame her for wanting to move on.

She just wished Rick would feel the same way.

As if summoned by her thoughts, their boss suddenly appeared in the doorway.

His face was lined with disgust, and she waited for him to inform the room that one of their newest hires had just been fired, but instead he said the last words she'd ever expect to come out of his mouth.

"It's with a heavy heart that I have to inform you that *The Benton Girls Revue* has just been cut from The Benton's line-up of shows."

Stunned silence met his announcement until Pru stuttered out, "You—you mean tonight's show has been cut? Just tonight's show, right?"

Rick shook his head. "I'm sorry, Pru, honey. I wish I could say it was just for tonight, or that management was just cutting back the number of shows we put on. I suggested all of that and even offered to take a pay cut. But Mr. Benton's assistant wasn't hearing any of it. She said *The Revue* is cancelled. No more shows— not even a farewell one. Order came from The Third himself."

Cole Benton III or "The Third" as some of the longer-time employees called him. Sunny had never met the CEO of The Benton Group herself, but according to Nora, he wasn't anything like his grandmother, all work and no play with little to no sense of humor. Still, Sunny wouldn't have expected this from The Third. His grandmother had started out a showgirl and surely he knew how much Nora treasured *The Revue*. Not only was the theater they performed in named after her, but she also came to see the show the second Tuesday of every month, and she'd even had the Benton Girls perform at her annual Christmas event to raise money for Lung Cancer awareness, which had taken the lives of both Sunny's grandmother and Nora's husband.

As if reading Sunny's mind, Rick said, "Sunny, aren't you besties with Nora Benton?"

"Not exactly," Sunny answered. "She and my grandmother were very close friends."

"Sunny's grandmother was our first African-American showgirl here at The Benton, and then she went on to become one of our most prized seamstresses behind the scenes," Rick informed the group, his voice somber and reverent. He held his hand out palm up toward Sunny and said to the rest of the dancers, "So you see, Sunny has both a personal and a historical stake in making sure our show goes on, and we can continue the story her grandmother began."

Well, she wouldn't quite put it that way. Though Sunny was proud of her grandmother for integrating *The Benton Girls,* that didn't mean that she herself wanted to stay with the show forever like her grandmother had.

"Sure, I can give Nora a call," she offered. "Though I'm not sure how much she can do."

Rick waved his hand in front of his chest. "No, no, no. Not Nora. If she had any power in this organization, I'm sure we wouldn't even be having this conversation."

True, Sunny thought. Nora loved *The Revue.* If she had anything to say about it, *The Benton Girls* would have kept going forever.

"No, we need you to go to the top dog himself," Rick told her. "In person, so he can't just deflect your call. How about it, Sunny? Will you go plead our case with The Third? Figure out a way to keep one of the last revues in Vegas going, so we're not all out of a job?"

Sunny wanted to say no. She wasn't exactly a master negotiator.

However, everyone in the dressing room was looking at her now with beseeching eyes, including Pru, her best friend, who really needed this job and the benefits it provided to support both herself and her little brother.

"Okay," Sunny found herself saying against her better instincts. "I'll go talk to Mr. Benton. I'll go talk to him right now."

Chapter 3

The Benton Group currently had holdings all over the United States, but Cole Benton had maintained the flagship executive offices near the top of the hotel's original forty-story building. So Sunny didn't have to go far to confront The Third. After getting back into her street clothes and borrowing a cardigan from Pru to wear over her tank top, it was only a matter of simply walking on over to The Benton's main bank of elevators.

However, when she got inside the first elevator car that opened up for her and pushed the button for the 35th floor, her head began to fill with righteous steam. Seriously, how dare Cole Benton just cut their show without even a little bit of warning? *What a prick,* she she thought, as she walked past the empty receptionist desk, rehearsing the polite but passionate plea Rick had all but written down for her.

Sunny came to an abrupt pause in the doorway of the outer office. Then she checked the nameplate on the door. The wood-and-glass sign declared this to be the office of Cole Benton, the CEO of The Benton Group of Hotels and Casinos. However, his outer office was not only sparse, with just a simple black desk and a black leather couch to appoint it, but it was also empty, the chair behind the secretary's desk currently without an occupant.

Sunny hesitated, all revved up with nowhere to go. What should she do? Wait for the secretary on the couch? Hope that she'd be back sometime soon? Or...

Her eyes went to the closed door, which was painted black, as if Mr. Benton truly wanted a soul to think twice before entering his inner sanctum. And it worked. Sunny's stomach churned at the thought of actually going in there.

But she ignored the butterflies writhing around in her belly and concentrated on taking one step, then another, then a few more after that, until she could take no more. She was right at his office door now. She had no choice but to run away or to knock.

Her main instinct was to run away. She hadn't even worked up the nerve to tell Rick she was moving to New York. Did she really think she had what it took to confront Cole Benton face-to-face?

But she had to do this, she decided in the end. For Rick, and her coworkers, most of whom she considered friends. She took a deep breath and raised her hand for what she hoped would be a polite but firm knock on Mr. Benton's door.

Before her knuckles could touch the dark wood, the door swung open, and suddenly her field of vision was filled with a dark tie and a well-cut suit, covering what looked like a lean, well-muscled chest.

Her gaze traveled up. The man staring down at her had dark brown hair, a square chin and a set of green eyes so intense, they put her in mind of a hawk. She'd noticed his official corporate photo a few times downstairs in the lobby, him unsmiling with the hotel's famous choreographed water fountain in the background. Just looking at him standing there in front of shooting jets of water had made her feel cold, as if looking at a picture of a snow-peaked mountain.

But now standing in front of him, his eyes were just as icy as they'd been in the photo. However, this time his gaze didn't make Sunny feel cold. In fact, it burned into her, rooting her to the spot with electric attraction.

And maybe he was just as stunned by her appearance, because he also went still, as if someone had hit the pause button on his brain. But only for a moment, and then his crystal green gaze began a slow descent down her body…and all the words she had prepared suddenly flew out of her head.

They stared at each other like this for moments on end, him the hawk, her as scared and speechless as a mouse.

"Yes, what do you want?" he finally said, with only the slightest uplift on "want" to let her know this was actually a question. His voice was dark, precise—like a gun shooting bullets.

Sunny cleared her throat. "Hi….um, I'm—"

"I know who you are."

"Really?" The words came out as a squeak. She tried again. "Really?"

"Yes, really." He crooked his head as if he were trying to decode her, even though as far as Sunny knew, there was nothing to decipher. "My grandmother speaks very highly of you for some reason."

"Oh, Nora, of course," Sunny said, relaxing a bit at the sound of her friend's name. "That's so nice of her to say nice things about me. I've had a lot of fun helping her with the Christmas Lung Cancer event over the years. Though, I've, ah, never seen you at any of those events...."

This observation caused that green gaze of his to shutter. "No, I was too busy running the corporation that provides all the money for Nora's charity events."

This made Sunny's nose crinkle. "Too busy even for your grandma? I mean if my grandma were still alive and asked me to come out, anywhere, I'd make the time."

Cole's lips thinned. "I suppose we have different ways of showing our relatives we value them. I think keeping my grandmother rich beyond her wildest dreams is enough, whereas you seem to think I'm neglecting her if I don't show up at her little Christmas party."

Sunny shrugged. "Money's nice, for sure. Believe me, I know that," she said, thinking fleetingly of her dream to move to New York. "But if I had to choose between a big old pile of money, or family, I'd choose family every time."

Cole gave her a grumpy look. "I can see why she likes you if you go around spouting crap like that."

"Excuse me, it's not crap—" Sunny broke off before her temper could get away from her. Yes, Cole Benton was an ass who couldn't be bothered to support his own grandmother, but unfortunately, he was the ass who could get *The Benton Girls Revue* back up and running. She had to be nice to him.

"I'm sorry, Mr. Benton, I think we've gotten off on the wrong foot." She pasted on a smile and went back to the script Rick had gone over with her. "I'm actually here as a friend of your grandmother's to talk with you about your recent decision to cancel *The Benton Girls Revue.*"

Mr. Benton's mouth twisted up. "Oh, that," he said, his monotone making it clear how unenthused he was to pursue the particular topic of conversation. But then he surprised her by stepping back, and holding the door open for her. "I suppose you'd better come in."

She did, glancing around the mostly black-and-white room before tentatively sitting down on one of the hard black guest chairs. The whole office put her in mind of a chessboard, and she had the feeling that the association was intentional, as if to say to visitors, "once you step into Cole Benton's space it's game on."

And it became clear who was the king on this board when Cole Benton sat down in the much larger chair behind his white desk, steepling his hands over its glass cover. "Talk."

Sunny swallowed and folded her hands in her lap. "As you know, *The Benton Girls Revue* is one of the oldest revues in Vegas, and even though I know it comes with its share of costs, it does still break even."

"Barely," Cole added. "And I'm not a fan of breaking even, especially when there are plenty of other shows interested in that space. Shows that would cost less and bring in a higher profit."

"I understand," Sunny answered. "But when you

add in *The Revue's* long history, anyone can see that you can't put a money amount on its value."

"Only if they don't have an MBA," Cole answered. "I'm assuming you don't."

What. A. Jerk. What complete and total jerk, she thought, trying to keep the lid on her temper. "No one knows the value of that history more than I do. My grandmother was the first black Benton Girl, and it really makes me sad to think her legacy won't be able to continue on—"

"So that's how our grandmothers met?" Cole asked. "While kicking up their heels on the *Benton Girl* line?"

"Yes, and that's why—"

"Save it," Cole said with a bored expression. "You've way overestimated the nostalgia factor. I'm a businessman first and foremost in all things, so I don't care how old *The Benton Girls Revue* is. The fact is we'd make more of a profit selling the costumes and set pieces we've used in it than we would keeping the show going, and that's what I value most, the bottom line."

Sunny had tried. She'd really tried, but she couldn't hold her temper back any longer. "Look, Mr. Benton. I'm not here about your bottom line, I'm here about the *people* who signed on to do a job in good faith and then had the carpet pulled out from under them today. Good people."

The man behind the desk threw her a skeptical look. "Let me guess, good people like you."

"Yes, good people like me," she agreed. "I have no shame in admitting I need this job to hit my life goals. But also, good people like my best friend, Prudence, who has a younger brother she's supporting all by herself. Two weeks severance isn't going to cut it for her."

"Life goals like what?"

Sunny blinked, a little thrown off track by his response to her passionate speech. "What?"

"You said you have life goals that you need this job to support. What are they?"

Sunny frowned, all sorts of discombobulated. "You really want to know...?"

Mr. Benton heaved a huge sigh. "You've already seen how much I value the bottom line, so you should just assume that I also value my time, since it's worth a lot of money. Believe me, Ms. Johnson, I don't waste it with questions I don't want answered."

Sunny adjusted herself in the black chair. "All right. I haven't told Rick or your grandmother this yet, so I'd appreciate you keeping it to yourself until I do."

She paused, waiting for him to promise, but he just stared back at her. The king on his chessboard, refusing to make any concessions to a mere pawn.

"I recently received a scholarship to earn an MFA in dance pedagogy—that's basically like dance education—at New York Arts University. They'll cover my tuition in exchange for me agreeing to teach in their dance program for low-income neighborhoods for the two years that I'm there. But they don't provide room or board, and room and board isn't exactly cheap—even in the outer boroughs where I'd be living..."

"No, it isn't," he agreed, his voice thoughtful, like he'd never even considered how the other half lived before.

Probably because he hadn't, Sunny thought to herself before continuing on. "So you see why I need this job at least until August, along with all the other hard working dancers in *The Revue*."

For some reason, Mr. Benton smiled. Smiled like a Cheshire cat. "Yes, yes, I do see now."

She waited for him to expand on that statement, but he continued to sit there, his brow crinkled, like he was running some sort of calculation.

Sunny looked from side to side. "Does this mean you're actually thinking about not cancelling the show?"

"Depends," Mr. Benton answered.

"On what?" she asked when he once again fell quiet.

He sat forward. "On what you're willing to do to make sure the show goes on."

Chapter 4

Cole watched as the showgirl's eyes widened slightly, like a rabbit suddenly caught in a trap. He continued to study her every reaction, while calculating his next words. He could tell she was confused. Very confused, but he didn't rush in with an explanation. He hadn't gotten to the top of his business by not carefully evaluating each and every one of his business rivals before and after they sat down on his chessboard, and he considered this showgirl, Sunny Johnson, a business rival.

One who happened to be extremely sexy, with long legs and soft curves that made his hands itch to do more than talk business.

She was fascinating, not at all what he'd expected, not just because she was African-American—though Nora choosing someone outside their race for him to wed had certainly been a surprise. She was so opposite of most of the people he associated with in Vegas. Vegas was a town built on big gambles and everyone who worked there from CEOs to the guys who cleaned the pit floors tended to hold their cards close to the chest. But not this woman.

It was the wide-open expression that had really thrown him at first. Every emotion she felt shone clearly on her face. Starting with her initial attraction to him when they first met in his doorway, soon followed by her irritation and righteous indignation as she defended the jobs of her fellow dancers, and eventually careful pride when she told him about the little scholarship she'd gotten to NYAU.

In fewer than ten minutes, he'd figured out that she wasn't quite the parasitic gold digger he'd assumed she must be when Nora had first brought up her name. But then again, she wasn't exactly a helpless damsel in distress, either. He'd found that out when he tried to run roughshod over her pitch to save *The Benton Girls Revue* and gotten an earful back.

She wasn't jaded, but she wasn't easily manipulated, either. Cole valued frankness and candor in many of his business dealings. But in this case he had the feeling that straight-up asking her to help him deal with his grandmother's outrageous demand wouldn't go over too well, even if she truly did need money to fund her move to New York.

"My grandmother…she likes you a lot," he said carefully. Then he waited for her to respond.

"I like her, too," Sunny answered. "She's a wonderful woman, and she always made sure my grandmother had a place at The Benton. I'm fortunate to call her a friend."

Cole didn't know whether to be annoyed or impressed that his grandmother apparently wanted him to marry her biggest fan.

"Yes, she is an extraordinary woman." *Extraordinarily presumptuous,* he thought to himself. "And unfortunately, she's in declining health these days."

Declining mental health—and that was technically only Cole's opinion as of now, but tomato-to-mah-to.

Sunny's eyes widened and she seemed truly worried. "Oh, no, I'm sorry to hear that. I saw her at one of our shows last week and she seemed in perfect health. She never said anything."

Cole lowered his eyes, which he hoped was a good enough approximation of upset. It had been so long since he'd allowed himself to show any feeling at all during a business negotiation, he wasn't sure what it would even look like. "It's not something she likes to talk about. Her good days are pretty good, but her bad days…" He deliberately let that sentence trail off. "Her bad days aren't something I like to talk about, either."

Especially now, when he was trying to convince this showgirl that his tough-as-nails grandmother was in declining health.

He pushed forward to the next topic. "But you're right. I've been focused mainly on establishing The Benton Group as a national contender in the hotel industry over the last few years, but my grandmother had an episode this morning, and it made me realize, blood really is more powerful than money."

Especially when that blood holds more power than she should in your corporation, he thought with an inner glare. Why his grandfather had willed Nora so many shares without limiting her power to use them, he had no idea. But if and when he ever got married, Cole knew he wouldn't make the same error in judgment with his own wife.

Sunny put a hand over her chest and her eyes went soft as she said, "It is. It truly is. I miss my own grandma every day."

"Ms. Johnson, I'm just going to level with you. My grandmother doesn't have long. To the end of the year if she's lucky, and it's become important to me to make her happy during these next few months."

Sunny nodded. "Of course. I completely understand." She pursed her lips. "But how do you figure cancelling *The Revue* will make her happy?"

Cole kept his face composed while scrambling for an answer to her question. "The truth is cancelling the show was my way of trying to put some limits on her activities. I want her to get the rest she needs."

Sunny frowned. "Knowing Nora, she definitely wouldn't appreciate that."

"No, I suppose she wouldn't. But now that I know there's a sympathetic person on staff who knows about the situation, maybe I could see my way to reopening the show, at least for the next few months. Especially if it would make Nora happy."

Sunny sat forward, her eyes full of worry for his grandmother. "I will do anything to make sure she doesn't overdo it when she's visiting us."

"She won't appreciate being coddled," Cole warned her sharply.

"I know she won't. And I won't coddle her, I'll just make things easier for her, I promise. If you put the show back on, you won't regret it."

He nodded as if he were giving her idea of helping out serious consideration as opposed to leading her straight into his trap. "The only thing is that even the show isn't enough to make her happy these days. You won't believe what she— No, I don't want to drag you into this."

But Sunny shook her head. "No, tell me. Maybe I can help."

"You could, but it would be weird. I couldn't..."

"Please tell me, Mr. Benton."

Cole put a reluctant tone into his voice as he answered. "The thing is my grandmother is very fond of you."

He pretended to hesitate some more and waited for Sunny to prod him along, so that she could think this whole conversation was her idea.

"Yes, you told me that," she said, right on cue. "But what does that have to do with the state of her health?"

"She's so fond of you, that her wish—I guess you could call it her dying wish is that I..."

Again he stopped and waited.

Sunny was leaning all the way forward in her seat now, her pretty brown eyes wide with curiosity.

"That you what?" she asked.

"Marry you."

He could hear Sunny's breath catch, and he again went silent. Biding his time. Like the predator she had no idea he was when it came to business.

"Are you serious?" she finally asked after a few opens and closes of her mouth.

He laid a solemn hand on his chest. "Believe me, Ms. Johnson, I would never ever joke about something like this." Lie through his teeth, yes. But joke? Never.

"I don't...I don't know what to say."

"You don't have to say anything right now," he answered, his mind working furiously behind his calm eyes to figure out how to make this next thing sound less like a threat and more like a win-win for both of them. "You want something from me and I need something from you for my grandmother."

"You want me to help you trick her?" Sunny asked. He could practically see her struggling with her conscience.

It must be tiring to have one of those, he thought to himself. "I want you to help me make my grandmother happy," he rephrased.

"And making Nora happy...what would that entail?" Sunny's voice was hesitant, but Cole could tell she was mulling the idea over, which meant he was in.

He somehow kept the smirk off his face as he answered. "There would be a whirlwind romance for a couple of months, and then we'd announce our engagement—probably at one of my grandmother's events."

"Like her August Children's Charity ball?"

He pointed at her. "Perfect." Nora had been nagging him to attend that stupid event for years and this year it would be the weekend before the end of summer board meeting. Why not kill two birds with one stone?

"It would make Nora very happy to have us announce it there."

"And if I agreed to this...to making Nora happy, it would just be pretend, right? We wouldn't have to... be intimate. Would we?"

This time Cole let the silence drift on for much longer than he knew was suitable, even in business. He was aware this question was meant to be a deal closer. He should just say no, there wouldn't be anything intimate required and leave it at that—he knew that would be enough to close the deal and ensure that his playboy brother didn't get his grubby mitts on his business.

However, he found that he didn't want to make the woman sitting in front of him this guarantee. He surreptitiously let his gaze roam down her body. Her yoga pants and tank top combo, while not the jewel-covered bikini she was required to wear for *The Revue,* only seemed to accentuate her curves. An image of himself disrobing her, yanking that thin cardigan down her arms, and pulling that tank top over her head to reveal what lay underneath flashed into his mind.

He considered himself already married. To his job. The occasional discreet one-night stand arranged when he found that his other needs were getting in the way of his concentration at work. But obviously he'd let the time between one-night stands go too long, because he found himself suddenly unable to focus on the business at hand. Maybe Nora had been right about the needing to get laid part.

In any case, he found himself going off script to say, "Ms. Johnson, you are doing me a great favor, so this arrangement can be whatever you want it to be." He then asked her, "Do you want it to be intimate?"

Chapter 5

"Do you want it to be intimate?"

Sunny felt something catch in her throat and then there came a flood of emotion, suffusing not just her cheeks but also her entire body.

And though she barely knew the man, suddenly she was wondering what it would be like to kiss him. The lines of his face were so sharp and hard. Did they soften when he kissed a woman? What would his hands feel like on her body? She could almost feel them now, disappearing underneath Sunny's cardigan, pushing it off her shoulders—

Sunny! she chastised herself. *What are you thinking? Get it together, girl!*

Obviously she'd been single way too long. It had been a year since her breakup with Derek, the one that had inspired her to finally apply to grad school, and apparently the longtime drought was making her mind go to some seriously inappropriate places.

She averted her eyes, trying not to notice how rock solidly handsome Mr. Benton was in real life, how much hotter and sexier he read than his picture downstairs, as she answered, "I think it's probably best if we keep this strictly professional, don't you, Mr. Benton?"

Cole's face remained impassive, but she could sense him smirking behind those green eyes. "Professional it is behind closed doors, but you do understand that when we're out in public, we'll have to at least act intimate...for my grandmother's sake."

Sunny thanked the heavens for her melanin, because she could once again feel her cheeks burning. "Yes, I understand, Mr. Benton."

"Then perhaps you should call me Cole."

Sunny bit down on a rising panic, wondering how she'd come up here to fight for the survival of *The Benton Girls* and had somehow ended up agreeing to pose as Cole's fake girlfriend.

"I understand...Cole." His name felt foreign in her mouth. "What exactly would I be expected to do?" she asked him.

Strangely, this question was the one that finally drained the sexual tension out of the conversation. "Yes, good question," Cole said, leaning back in his chair, as if some spell had been broken and he was able to return to his businessman persona. "Let's talk terms..."

"What did you do?" Rick screamed when she came back to the Nora Benton theater about an hour later. He was on the phone, but that didn't stop him from catching Sunny up in a bear hug. "Sunny's here. I've got to go, but I'll see you for tonight's show. Six p.m. sharp," he yelled into the phone to whoever he had been speaking to.

When he hung up he looked at Sunny as if she were made of magic. "Cole Benton's secretary called a few minutes ago. She said the show was back on for at least another three months. How did you do it?"

Sunny shook her head, feeling sick to her stomach. "It's a long story," she said. "And you've probably got a lot of calls to make if you want to make the six o'clock call time. Maybe I can help you with that?"

"Oh, sweetie, would you?" Rick said, handing her the second sheet of the dancers' contact info list. "You truly are an angel. One of my best dancers and you got Benton to put the show back on. I still can't believe it."

"Actually, only one of those things are true now," Sunny said with a grimace. "I can't be one of your dancers anymore."

"What!" Rick responded to her announcement. His voice could probably be heard all the way on the pit floor, which only made Sunny more reluctant to go on. This was going to be way harder than quitting her cocktail waitress job, but she stuck to the script Cole had given her, even if it made her feel guilty as hell for outright lying to her stage dad.

"Well, Mr. Benton—ah, I mean Cole—said that he'd bring the show back, but he'd need someone to help him with his grandmother, Nora, and he offered me the job."

"So you're going to be Nora Benton's caretaker now?" Rick asked.

"No, not exactly. Technically, I'll be her assistant.

I'll be accompanying her to the show every month, helping her plan her August charity ball. Stuff like that."

"Why does Nora Benton suddenly need an assistant?" Rick asked. "She has more connections in Vegas than pretty much anybody else on the planet, and she's a total control freak. She's never needed any assistance before. What's changed..."

Rick's voice trailed off, then his eyes widened. "But The Benton Group doesn't allow its employees to date. Cole Benton wants into your pants! That's why he agreed to put the show back on, but made you take a job as his grandmother's assistant. He's into you!"

Sunny felt her cheeks warm for the third time in as many hours. Seriously, she was beginning to long for the days when the most embarrassing thing she did was wear a rhinestone bikini every night on stage. "I'm sure that's not it," she said, trying to keep her voice as demure as possible, despite knowing that was exactly what Cole Benton wanted people to believe, and that Rick was already playing right into his made-up story of a whirlwind romance.

"And I'm sure it is," Rick said. "But I'm not going to complain. You got the show back on, so I'm happy. Good job, Sunny!"

"Um...thank you, I guess," Sunny said, trying to decide whether she should be offended that Rick was more than willing to pimp her out to what he believed to be a predatory new boss if it kept *The Revue* going.

Rick soon redeemed himself with a sad look. "But baby girl, I have no idea how I'm going to replace you. I mean who's going calm the dancers down enough to go onstage after I finish screaming at them?"

Sunny threw him a surprised look. "You knew I was doing that?"

"Of course I did," Rick said. "I'm like God, I know everything that goes on in my backstage. But seriously, I'm going to need a name. I've got a doozy of a rant I've been writing out in my head for weeks, and I'm pretty sure there's going to be tears from some of the newbies. Do you think Pru can handle backstage mama duties?"

Sunny laughed. "I think she's ready, I really do."

"She better be!"

Sunny had to give her incorrigible boss a warm hug then. "I'm going to miss you so much, Rick," she said, meaning it.

"Me, too, sweetheart." Then he leaned back, and held his finger up. "Go take one for the team with Cole Benton, but be careful with that one. He's good lookin', but he's a shark. Don't let your heart get involved or he'll eat you alive."

A chill ran down Sunny's spine. She had the feeling she should be taking Rick's warning seriously, even though she was the one who'd agreed to help out Cole.

Chapter 6

On Tuesday morning Sunny had two jobs. By Tuesday afternoon, she only had one…and no idea what to do with herself. Her new job was pretty much fake, a cover story to get around The Benton Group's non-fraternization policy, which would hopefully help sell their whirlwind romance. Though Cole Benton didn't exactly strike her as a whirlwind-romance type of guy. Their first date wasn't scheduled until Sunday night, some business dinner, which she didn't even have to shop for, because Cole's secretary had emailed that she'd be sending over a dress for the event. So she had a lot of time on her hands. A lot of time.

The first few days, she spent deep cleaning her entire apartment and setting up a bunch of traps for the rat who'd stolen her meal replacement bar. There were no signs of him in the cabinets, thank goodness, but she doubted she'd seen the last of him. Quite frankly her apartment was a dump, chosen shortly after she and Pru had given up their lease due to Pru's parents dying in a car accident and her having to take over as her high-school-aged brother's only guardian. Sunny's apartment was cramped and in a questionable neighborhood, but it was also cheap and right on a major bus route, so she never had any trouble getting to work. The good had outweighed the bad—until her furry roommate had showed up.

After that it hadn't been worth the amount of sleep she'd lost, because she kept jerking awake, thinking she heard the quick movement of tiny feet inside her walls.

By the time Saturday night rolled around, Sunny was a wreck, still tired, and bored on top of it. But for the first Saturday night in her working life, she had no boss to report to, no dances to perform or drinks to serve, no friends to go out with since they all were *Benton Girls* performers—nothing to do but twiddle her thumbs.

She'd already read every book in her apartment, and choreographing a whole new routine for her Sunday girls' dance class at the Balzar Community Center had only occupied her time for a few hours. By five, she was nearly out of her mind with boredom, and thinking she should use some of her hard saved money to buy a TV. Something she'd never bothered with before, because she was usually too exhausted to do much more than fall into bed when she got home from either of her jobs.

People call New York the city that never sleeps, but really it was Vegas that never shut down, not even for national holidays, not for one single neon weekend. There was always work to do in Vegas. But here she was now with nothing to do.

Just then her doorbell rang, and she was more than a little surprised to see who was standing on the other side of the door when she opened it.

Before she could even work up a pleasant hello, Cole Benton held up a manila envelope. "Your confidentiality agreement," he said. He looked very, very annoyed. Even though he was the one who had shown up at her front door unannounced.

"You want me to sign a contract?" she asked, blinking as she tried to catch up.

"Yes," he answered, then he pushed past her, barging into her apartment without invitation.

"Please come right on in," she said, closing the door behind him:

He either didn't pick up on her sarcasm or didn't care. He looked around the apartment for a few seconds, then he pulled the contract out of the envelope. "Sign there and there. It's pretty standard. You won't say anything about any of this to anyone, including Nora."

Sunny wondered if she'd ever get used to hearing him call his grandmother by her first name. She knew her own grandma wouldn't have put up with that even for a second. But she had the feeling The Third—she meant, *Cole*—probably got away with a lot of behavior most people couldn't.

She signed on the line above her printed name, "You couldn't have just mailed this to me?" she asked. "I thought we weren't supposed to start pretending to date until tomorrow night…"

She trailed off when she saw that Cole wasn't listening, instead his phone was to his ear.

"What time do you think you can have the moving truck meet us here?"

"Wait, why is a moving truck coming here?" she demanded.

Cole kept talking as though she hadn't said anything. "Couple of hours? Great." He then frowned at something the person on the other side of the phone had said. "I don't know. I'll ask her."

He lowered the phone and glanced at Sunny. "Do you want the movers to pack you up? Or do you want to do that yourself?"

Sunny screwed up her face. "What? When did I agree to move?"

Cole put the phone back up to his ear. "She's not sure. Just tell whoever you get to be ready for an either-or situation. I'll touch base later. Thanks."

As soon as he hung, she informed him, "I'm not moving to…" She realized she had no idea where he was trying to make her go, and finished with a tepid, "Wherever you're trying to make me move."

Cole picked up the signed contract and flipped through it before turning the found page around and pointing to a paragraph. Sunny read it. Something about her agreeing not to do or say anything that would cast him in the bad light.

"How is living in my own apartment casting you in a bad light?" she asked.

He shook his head. "No man of my standing would ever let his girlfriend live in a dump like this."

"It's not that bad," Sunny argued, her voice sounding a little weak even to her own ears, as she tried to keep her eyes from straying over to the water stains on the walls.

"It's a dump," he repeated. "And judging from the deal I saw going down in the nearby stairwell, probably not at all safe. You move in with me until my assistant can set you up in a decent apartment."

Sunny's first thought was to argue with him. No one told her what to do or where to live.

But then the image of the rat with her protein bar in its mouth floated across her mind. She could still hear distinctly the high-pitched click-suck of its teeth.

"Exactly where would this apartment be?" she asked. "It would have to be something I could afford on my own."

"That's something you can discuss with Agnes when the time comes," he said, sounding brusque and bored with this whole line of conversation.

Sunny tried not to bristle. She supposed she should just be grateful he hadn't decided to make a big deal of her easy acquiescence. "I... Um. Don't really need a moving truck," she mumbled. "Everything I have fits easily into two suitcases. I've been getting rid of a bunch of things before I go to New York."

He brought out his phone and started texting. "All right, I'll have Agnes call off the moving truck. Pack up and I'll drive you back to my place."

"You don't have to drive me—"

He cut her off with another disapproving stare. "If your car is anything like your apartment, I think I do."

She thought of the bus, which had served her well over the year she'd been living there. "The bus gets the job done," she said, feeling the need to defend Las Vegas's transit system.

Cole didn't even look up from his smartphone. "I'm telling Agnes to pull out one of the cars from my garage. You can probably handle the Mercedes."

"Really, you don't have to—"

Cole crossed his arms across his chest. "So is the plan to keep me waiting instead of packing your bags quickly?"

Sunny pursed her lips. Cole was acting as if everything he was commanding was the most logical thing ever, but she wasn't a doormat.

"You know you've got me thinking…" she said.

His eyes narrowed, but he remained quiet, waiting for her to go on. He seemed to have two modes of communicating, Sunny noted to himself. Either issuing commands or using silence in a way that felt as though he were carefully wielding a weapon.

She continued on, anyway, even further convinced by his weaponized silence that she should try to gain some sort of upper hand. "You're trying to sell us as a couple, and that's why you want me in an apartment I probably couldn't afford on my own and driving a nicer car than I would buy if I had one. Obviously, you're used to dating a certain type, and I'm not it."

"No, you're not my usual type," he agreed. However, a heat sprung up in his eyes when he added, "You're not like anyone I've ever dated. But I don't think I'm going to have any problems convincing others that I'd be more than willing to take you on as a lover."

His clipped words actually felt like a compliment. A rather sexy one, but Sunny forced herself to stay on her original course. "That's great," she said. "But the problem is you're not my type, either. The people in my circle—including Nora—might find it hard to believe I'm really with you. Like not just a fling, but seriously into you with the possibility of getting married."

The heat drained out of his gaze. "What exactly is your type, Sunny?" he asked and she felt a chill go up her back.

"Well, my last serious boyfriend ran a homeless shelter. We met while he was asking people to sign up to volunteer there, outside of Trader Joe's."

Cole crooked his head, like the whole idea of actually doing good in the world was a completely foreign concept to him.

Maybe it was, Sunny thought unkindly, wondering, not for the first time how she'd ever gotten herself into this mess.

"You're saying you'd prefer that I'd be more charitable," Cole concluded. "Fine. Tell me what charity you like, and I'll have Agnes make a donation."

She gave him a leveled look. "I was actually thinking more charitable, like doing. Like if people saw us doing charitable things together, maybe they wouldn't have such a hard time buying my story."

Cole crinkled his forehead. "So you want us to spend time together, helping people. Fine, I can do that? Tell me how."

"I guess you could come with me to my community dance class tomorrow. It's all girls, and we're always looking for guys to help us with lifts."

"What time?"

"Seven—I know that's early. But a lot of my girls are Catholic, and have to be done in time for second Mass at St. Peter's."

Cole brought his phone back out and started typing. "It's not early for me. I'll have Agnes clear my schedule."

Now it was her turn to shake her head. "You work on Sunday mornings, too?"

"Of course I do," he answered, like she was the odd one because she didn't.

Chapter 7

Sunday morning, Cole woke up way earlier than usual, and in a foul mood. He'd tossed and turned the entire night, a certain part of his anatomy reminding him with increasing insistence that Sunny was now living in the penthouse apartment he kept at the top of The Benton. Living with him. She was right there, in the very next bedroom, her soft, curvaceous body lying underneath a couple of sheets and a thin blanket, which he'd only have to pull back to...

He'd been forced to take care of himself around 3:00 a.m. like a high school boy, and even that hadn't been enough. Now he was wide-awake with a mind that didn't want to shut back down.

With an aggrieved grunt, he got out of bed. His master bedroom, and the rest of his penthouse were done up like his office downstairs, with white floors and walls, and sleek black furniture. However, the chessboard feel of the place didn't give him his usual satisfaction, because whatever was going on with Sunny, it didn't feel like he was currently winning. Even though the house was always supposed to win, and he was the CEO of the house.

He went into his home office, which was located right across the hallway from his bedroom to get a head start on the work he'd normally be doing on a Sunday morning, if he hadn't agreed to accompany Sunny to her silly dance class.

"Are you seriously working at five-thirty on a Sunday morning?" he heard her ask behind him a couple of hours later.

He turned around to give her a peevish answer about the difference in income levels between him and the guys who didn't work on Sunday mornings, but the words got stuck in his mouth as he studied her appearance in his office doorway.

He was used to the type of women who slipped out of bed before he did to fix their hair and makeup. Sometimes they even spritzed on a little perfume.

But Sunny looked as if she'd just climbed out of a tumble dryer, rumpled clothes, glossy curls going every which way, including up. However, that combined with her bountiful curves, barely contained by the drawstring pants and tank top she'd worn to bed sent a lightning bolt of lust straight through him.

Instead of putting her in her place, he had to work hard to keep the physical strain out of his voice. "Did you need something?" Other than him inside of her, right now?

"Coffee," she all but groaned. "I can't even think about a shower until I've had at least one cup."

He couldn't remember the last time a woman had even dared to approach him for anything other than morning sex without having taken a shower first—and often not even that. No, Sunny was definitely not his usual type. Not even remotely.

Yet, he had to turn around in his swivel chair for fear of what his smaller brain would compel him to do if he had to look at her another second.

"In the kitchen. It's an automatic pot. The housekeeper sets it up every day."

"Thanks," she said to his back. "Can I bring you back a cup—"

"No," he answered, before she could even finish asking the question.

"Okay," she said carefully. Then she mercifully walked away, giving him the time he needed to get himself back under control.

He was still in a bad mood when he followed Sunny into the Balzar Community Center, which was located in an area of Las Vegas he'd only visited how many times? Oh, wait, that would be never, because he'd never had any reason to test out the fallibility of his Lo Jack system.

"Your car will be fine," Sunny teased, apparently reading his mind as they walked through the building's front door.

She'd had the nerve to come out to the living room dressed in a pink leotard, tights and leg warmers. She was either better at hiding her intentions than he'd originally given her credit for, or she honestly had no idea what the sight of someone with her kind of curves dressed in an outfit like that could do to a man.

Either way, he took a moment to resent the hell out of her for making it so he could barely look at her, because he was working so hard at keeping himself from tenting his pants. It didn't help that she looked happy and in good spirits, like she'd gotten the best sleep of her life, while he'd tossed and turned all night.

And now she was teasing him about worrying about his Bentley, which probably cost more than this entire building.

Time to teach his pawn a lesson and put himself back in control of the chessboard, he decided.

"We're early," he pointed out as Sunny led him down a narrow hallway with paint peeling off the walls. "Is there a reason for that?"

Sunny shook her head, "No, it just worked out that way—"

She broke off with a squeak when he took her by the waist and pressed her back into the one area of wall where the paint was still smooth. He let his body settle into hers, reveling in her softness, as he breathed in her scent. Shower gel and the apple she'd eaten for breakfast.

"What—what are you doing?" she asked him, her voice breathless with confusion…and something else.

He liked the something else part. Liked it a lot.

"We're supposed to be making our debut as a couple tonight at the Businessperson of the Year dinner."

"And that has what to do with you holding me against this wall?" she asked, looking incredibly uncomfortable, but also still…something else.

"We're supposed to be in the throes of a new romance, madly in love. Now I don't usually do PDAs. Not really my thing, but in this case, if I were really capable of falling hard for somebody in a matter of days, I think I'd be okay with it. Don't you?"

He could distinctly see a bead of sweat on her forehead now. "Are you hot, Sunny? Already? We haven't even begun the class. Maybe we should turn on the air conditioning," he offered, not even trying to hide the fake tone in his suggestion.

"No, I'm fine, I—" she broke off, obviously flustered. "I just don't understand what tonight has to do with right now. What you're doing right now?"

"We've got fifteen minutes. Maybe we should practice."

Before she could ask "practice what," he answered the presumed question, pressing his lips to hers for what was supposed to be a teasing kiss. A light punishment for giving him a hard time about his car and work schedule.

Except it wasn't teasing or light. In fact, when his lips met hers he felt something zap through him, and he immediately became consumed, moving his mouth over hers, wanting more. He pressed his whole body into her as he kissed her now, suddenly not caring if she knew how badly she affected him. Suddenly wanting her to know just how much he desired her, just how much he wanted in.

And apparently he wasn't the only one affected by their kiss. Her hand came around his neck, telling him by the way she pressed herself forward into his erection that she wanted him as much as he wanted her.

"Oohhhh! Teacher's got a boyfriend! Teacher's got a boyfriend!"

The teasing voice brought him back to reality. And then came Sunny's hands, abruptly pushing him away. He looked down, way down to see a young Latina girl, her hair arranged in a messy bun, pointing at them as she singsonged, "Teacher's got a boyfriend," over and over again.

"Lucia!" Sunny all but groaned as she slipped out from between him and the wall. What had she been thinking, letting him kiss her like that right before class? She'd obviously lost her entire mind.

No, she corrected herself, Cole had very purposefully gone out of his way to make it so that she couldn't think straight. She threw an angry sideways look at the man who had taken her by surprise, kissing her with more passion than she would have thought him capable of. Certainly more passion than her last boyfriend, who for all his altruistic attributes, had been more of a peck/no tongue kind of guy when it came to public displays of affection.

It felt as though she was both reminding herself and informing Lucia, when she said, "This is my *friend* Cole—"

"You mean your boyfriend! You mean your boyfriend!" Lucia sang back.

Cole arched his eyebrow, smirking as if he along with Lucia had just caught Sunny in an obvious lie.

Sunny's fingers came up to her temple and rubbed. "Lucia, I'm sorry you saw that. But I'd appreciate if you kept it to yourself. I don't want the rest of the class to get distracted—"

Once again, Lucia interrupted her, this time by puckering up and making kissing noises as she wrapped her arms around her shoulders and panto-mimed kissing.

Cole raised the other eyebrow. "And you chose this form of charitable work, because…?"

She was beginning to wonder that herself. She usu-ally enjoyed teaching her students, especially the imp-ish Lucia, whose wicked sense of humor occasionally derailed the class, but most often kept them laughing. However, the notion of Lucia telling everybody about the kiss she just witnessed had Sunny cringing.

"Please, Lucia…" Sunny said, only to be cut off when Lucia started making even louder kissing sounds.

Sunny opened her mouth to once again try reason-ing with the little girl, but this time it was Cole who cut her off.

"I'll give you ten bucks to keep your mouth shut, kid," he told Lucia.

And before Sunny could chastise him for bribing a child, Lucia brought the kissing sounds to an abrupt stop and said, "Thirty. You look like you got money. You can afford it."

"I've got money, because I don't let myself get swindled," Cole replied evenly. "Twenty."

Lucia folded her arms. "That your car outside?"

Cole, who didn't seem to recognize the difference between a fellow businessman and child, narrowed his eyes as though he suspected Lucia might be try-ing to pull one over on him. "Yeah, that's my car," he said carefully.

"Give me a ride home in it, and I'll take the twenty."

"Fine," Cole said. "What's your full name, kid?"

"Lucia. Lucia Reyes," she answered.

Cole held out his hand, stiff as a general. "Lucia Reyes, we've got a deal, but if you break your promise, I'm going to make sure this dance class gets shut down and you never have anybody to teach you to twirl around for free again, because you couldn't keep your mouth closed."

"Cole!" Sunny admonished.

But before Sunny could speak another word, Lucia said, "Deal! And you won't have to shut us down. I don't snitch!" She took his hand and shook it firmly, while Cole smirked at Sunny over the little girl's head.

When Cole had agreed to help Sunny with her class, he'd thought, *sure, why not? How hard could it be?*

The answer was, pretty damn hard.

Cole ran an extreme amount of miles three times a week and did a brutal strength workout every Tuesday and Thursday, but helping Sunny teach her free dance class on Sunday nearly did him in. The pliés alone seemed to be working muscles none of his squat sessions had ever addressed. And though he'd done Arnold presses with dumbbells that weighed more than the girls in Sunny's dance class, dumbbells didn't wiggle or giggle when Sunny yelled at him. "You can do better than that, Benton. Get her higher!"

The unassuming showgirl who'd walked into his office became a complete harridan in the little dance studio, yelling at both him and the girls. It felt as though their jumps were never high enough, their arms never straight enough. And even when he'd thought they'd done something perfectly, she'd just bang her stick on the ground and yell, "Again!"

"Now I know why you volunteer," he grumbled

as they left the building with Lucia following behind them. Lucia was making a big production of their exit, giving the other girls a swanning wave as she informed them she'd be riding home in *the Bentley*.

Cole ignored Lucia's antics, instead turning to Sunny as he said, "I can't see anyone actually paying you to put them through that kind of abuse."

Sunny just smiled at him. Apparently yelling at him and sixteen little girls for an hour had energized her in a way that her pre-shower cup of coffee hadn't. "I challenge them, and when they're done with my class they leave with a feeling of accomplishment. That's something money can't buy."

"Everything can be bought." He jerked his thumb at Lucia, who'd taken it upon herself to open the door to the Bentley and climb into the backseat, no invitation needed. "That's a fact of life. You just have to figure out the price."

She returned his look with a sharp one of her own, and he could see she was trying to figure out if he was still talking about the proverbial sense of accomplishment...or something else.

Cole decided to make it easy for her. He leaned down and whispered in her ear, "That was one hell of a kiss, Sunny, and before this is all done, I'm going to figure out what it will take to get you in my bed."

She let out a soft gasp, but before she could answer or slap him, he opened the passenger door for her. Like the gentleman he definitely wasn't.

Chapter 8

Cole Benton had misled everyone. He wasn't boring, or frozen, or stiff—in fact, he was a very, very dangerous man. Sunny realized this way too late. After she was fully installed in his apartment, and after she'd already agreed to go to the Businessperson of the Year dinner as his date.

And she cursed herself for being so late on the penny drop as she found herself alone with him once again after they got into Cole's private elevator to go back up to his penthouse.

Or at least *she* would be riding the elevator back to his penthouse suite. Cole pushed the button for the 35th floor.

"You're going straight into the office?" she asked, eyeing his sweats.

"I have a shower in my personal bathroom," he answered. "And an extra suit."

"Oh, that's...nice."

The doors whispered closed and Cole gave her a sideways glance. "I'll be back in time to escort you to the dinner."

"Okay, good, good," Sunny answered, not really knowing how to talk to him after what he'd said to her before they'd gotten into his car.

An image of Cole kissing her against the community center's wall, his hands in her hair, his hard rigid length pressed against her, came crashing into her head, creating all sorts of inner havoc before Sunny shook her head to force it out. *No, Sunny, no, you can't let yourself go there just because you're a little more horny than usual these days.*

"Everything okay?" Cole asked.

"Everything's fine," she answered, pretending her breasts hadn't grown heavy with—something she didn't really want to think too hard about—but the longer they were in the small enclosed space together... the more her body stirred.

Yes, she needed to get back to the penthouse. That was definitely where she wanted to be. She needed some time with her own thoughts, and she needed to figure out how to get out of this arrangement without hurting Nora.

"You're thinking about that kiss," Cole said, his voice low and husky beside her.

Sunny's heart dropped into her stomach. How had he known?

"No," she lied.

"So am I," he told her as if she hadn't denied it.

"I wasn't..." she began.

Suddenly she found her back against the elevator

wall, with Cole pressed up against her front. "Sunny, here's something you don't know about me," he said, his breath hot against the side of her face. "I hate when people lie to me. So unless you want me to do what I've wanted to do ever since you came out of your room this morning, don't. Don't deny it."

Sunny swallowed, feeling as if all the moisture had suddenly run screaming out of her mouth. "I—I was thinking about the kiss," she admitted, deeply aware of his rigid length against her leg. "About how inappropriate it was…"

"Sunny— No look at me, Sunny," he said when she tried to avert her eyes. "You kissed me back," he reminded her.

Not that she needed the reminder. "Yes, I did, and that was…wrong." She swallowed again. "Really wrong."

Silence, and even though she really did avert her eyes this time, staring at the elevator's stainless-steel ceiling, she could still feel his eyes on her, as precise as a tractor beam. Then he moved against her.

Sunny let out a gasp of surprise, when his rigid length found her core, rocking against her so that despite the leotard she was wearing, she felt him from the bottom of her cleft all the way to the sensitive button at the top of it. And damn her traitorous body, her entire core suddenly filling up with the sweet ache of sexual need.

"Cole…" She meant for it to be a reprimand, but it came out as a helpless breath. Even to her own ears it sounded less as though she was chastising him and more as though she was begging for him.

The elevator dinged, and reality came crashing

back down around Sunny. What was she doing? How could she have let the situation get so far out of hand? *Again?* Because shame of all shames, she knew if that elevator hadn't dinged, she would have let Cole in, let him get it right there in the elevator with nothing but a small breath of nonprotest.

She put her hands on his chest and pushed. "Here's your floor," she told him. "You better go now before the doors close."

For a moment, she thought he might ignore her. He was breathing hard and she could feel him impossibly hard against her own sex. But just as the elevator doors were about to close, he stepped back from her and waved his hand between them, sending the two pieces of steel flying back open.

He cupped his hand around the elevator's inside frame, forcing the doors to stay open, and Sunny allowed herself an inner sigh of relief. Now he was on the other side of the elevator and out of touching range, so she was safe from him and the frightening level of desire he'd managed to spark within her with lightening speed. Twice.

But her relief was short-lived. His green gaze stayed on her as sure as a touch, for an alarmingly long time. So long, the elevator started to ding with irritation.

"I take that back," he said. His words were quiet, but Sunny was able to hear them perfectly despite the elevator's incessant ringing. "I hate when people lie to me, but I don't mind when you do. It's going to make it that much more fun when I make you take back every word."

Then and only then did he step out of the elevator. But he continued to stare at her, his eyes as cold and hard as the steel doors closing in front of him.

* * *

The memory of the stunned look on Sunny's face as the elevator doors closed made it hard for Cole to concentrate on his work. Too hard. He found himself reading over the same report from the efficiency firm he'd hired to look over The Benton Kansas City again, and he still couldn't say for sure whether the report was good or bad.

Not very efficient. Not very efficient at all.

He had to get his mind off Sunny, the way that pink leotard had covered all her lush curves without leaving anything to the imagination, the way her full lips had felt underneath his, the way she'd responded to him—before the dance class and in the elevator...

"Will you be needing anything else today, Mr. Benton?"

Cole looked up to see his assistant, Agnes, standing in the doorway, her dark eyes looking askance behind her round glasses. Confusion replaced his erotic thoughts. Was Agnes leaving early? That wasn't like her. After losing two assistants to claims of needing work–life balance, he'd explained to Agnes from the start that he needed an assistant who'd be available to him from six to six, not only on weekdays, but also on weekends, and even later if an important project came up. Agnes had answered that she really wanted this job, and that she'd let her husband, a construction worker named Steve, know what would be required of her.

But lately she'd seemed a bit worn down, like his seven-day-a-week schedule was taking a toll on her, and maybe her marriage. He'd overheard enough whispered phone conversations with her husband to know that Steve wasn't exactly on board with how many hours Cole required Agnes to work. But Cole kept his work life separate from his personal one, and he'd trusted Agnes to do the same, no matter how much her husband whined about it. Yet here she was trying to leave work early for the first time since he'd hired her and without asking permission ahead of time.

However, when Cole's eyes found the clock on the wall, he realized he was the one in the wrong. It was six o'clock. Which meant he'd just spent the past two hours looking over the same report and trying not to think about Sunny.

Unsuccessfully.

He cursed under his breath.

"Is everything okay, Mr. Benton?" Agnes asked, looking worried.

"No, it's fine," he answered, rubbing a hand over his face. "I just…didn't get as much done as I wanted to today."

"Oh," Agnes said. "Well, I can stay if you'd like. You have your Businessperson of the Year dinner tonight, but if you'd like, I can call Sunny and let her know you won't be able to make it. I was planning to give her a ring before I went home, anyway, to make sure she was fully satisfied with her hotel room."

Cole went still. Very still. "What hotel room?"

Chapter 9

Sunny pulled on the silk sheath dress that Agnes had arranged to have delivered to her new room just a few hours ago. How she knew Sunny's dress and shoe size, Sunny had no idea. She was just glad to be wearing an outfit that wasn't designed to put her cleavage and butt cheeks on full display, and which didn't contain a metric ton of rhinestones. No, this dress was black and slightly on the demure side with a lace bodice that only hinted at Sunny's breast size, but didn't point it out with neon signs.

Not quite the yoga pants and tank top ensembles she favored during her off hours, but Agnes had done well. The dress looked exactly like what someone Cole Benton was dating would wear. Stately and subtly sexy—but not too sexy.

Speaking of too sexy...embarrassment washed over

her as she opened the box with the chandelier earrings. What had happened in the elevator with Cole—well, it just shouldn't have. She still had no idea how or why it did. Why she had let it.

But she was sure of one thing: asking Agnes to put her up in one of The Benton's empty hotel rooms until she could find a suitable apartment for Sunny to move into was probably the smartest thing she'd done since applying to grad school. Sure she felt a little guilty about the extra expense. Okay, a lot guilty. Even with her employee discount, Sunny knew that even a standard room at The Benton was way out of her price range. But at least she was on the third floor of the hotel now. Nearly as far away from Cole Benton as she could get without leaving the building.

A loud banging knock sounded on the door, interrupting her thoughts.

"Sunny, it's Cole Benton," the heavy knocker said on the other side of the door, his words full of angry grit and gravel.

Sunny winced as she went over to the door and called back, "Oh, there must have been some kind of miscommunication. I'm still getting dressed, and I told Agnes to tell you I'd just meet you in the lobby at seven. So…" She let the sentence trail off, hoping he'd get the hint and go away.

He didn't go away. He definitely did not go away. Not only did Sunny not hear any footsteps but she could also sense him standing still on the other side of the single piece of wood that stood between them. A few beats ticked by. "Sunny, open the door," he said in a voice so menacing, she actually took a step back.

"Why?" she asked the door. "There's nothing to

talk about. I'm staying here until Agnes finds me a new apartment. End of conversation. I've made my decision."

Silence.

"Don't make me go down to the front desk and get a key card for your room. It will be worse if you do."

Worse than what? Her whole body began to tremble.

Why? She had no idea. It wasn't as if she wasn't used to facing down an audience, some of whom would yell out rather colorful commentary as she danced. Cole Benton was just another heckler, she told herself, one obviously hell-bent on making her uncomfortable just because he could. But what right did he have to threaten her? Or act like she had to do everything he said?

She would open the door, she decided, but not because he told her to—she'd do it to give him a piece of her mind. She wasn't going to let him intimidate her, she thought as she pulled open the door.

He came through the doorway like a rushing bull, fusing his mouth to hers with such force that she would have fallen backward if his arms hadn't come around her tighter than steel bands.

It all happened fast after that.

He lifted her off her feet and slammed her against the hotel room door, which had swung closed on its own.

"Are you trying to drive me crazy?" he demanded against her mouth, before kissing her again with bruising force. Then he stated it as fact. "You're trying to drive me crazy."

"No, I'm not," Sunny insisted, even as she let her

neck fall back to receive his lips there, as well. "I would never... Believe me, I was just trying to put some distance between us, so this—this wouldn't happen again."

His eyes collided with hers, harsh and unforgiving. "Listen to me, Sunny. Listen hard. This—" he pointed between the two of them "—this is happening. I don't know what you thought you would accomplish when you tricked Agnes into giving you a room in my hotel behind my back, but all you did was make the inevitable come even faster. Now you've pissed me off."

He stood back and ripped her dress down the front. Actually ripped it! And before she could gasp, he caught her response with another hard kiss, his hand finding the V between her legs, cupping it as though it belonged to him, even as he growled, "You're not wearing underwear. Bullshit, you're not trying to drive me crazy."

His hand was so hot on her sex, she squirmed not knowing quite what to do. "No, I just hadn't put them on yet. I told you I wasn't finished getting dressed—"

She broke off with another gasp when one hand locked around her wrists, pinning them above her head on the wall. Meanwhile two of his fingers pushed into her with sharp intent.

He looked at her, his eyes as cold as gravestones. "Here's what's going to happen now, Sunny. You're going to get wet, as wet as you need to be to take me inside of you. All of me inside you."

As if under his thrall, her body responded to his command. Sunny whimpered, and she could actually feel herself creaming with desire, as she clenched and unclenched around his fingers.

"All of me all the way inside of you," he growled in her ear.

The feel of his fingers pumping in and out of her. So wrong. So not what she should be doing with this man. It was too much, and she could already feel a climax building up inside of her. "No..." Sunny moaned.

Cole's hand came to an abrupt stop. "Don't tell me no."

"We shouldn't," Sunny gasped out, even as her hips rolled against his now still hand, seeking the sensations he'd taken away when he stopped.

Cole tutted. "Sunny, Sunny, Sunny...you're beautiful and you're sexy as hell, but you're a terrible liar. Your mouth is telling me one thing while your body is telling me another."

Sunny was deeply aware of the contradiction. And she tried to still her body. Make it stop, but she was too far gone. "Please..." she pleaded trying to gain control of the movement of her hips.

"Please what, Sunny?" he said. "Please stop or please go on?"

Stop, stop, stop! Tell him to stop! the little sense she had left screamed at her. But out loud she said, "Go on...I need—"

He was giving it to her before she could even complete the request, his fingers once again plunging in and out, even faster now, as if he knew exactly where she was at, that she was almost there. "Don't tell me no again. That's the last one you get. Now come for me, Sunny."

He was out of his mind. She was sure of it. But the orgasm hit her hard, rushing through her with a sweet ache, and momentarily quelling the raging desire he'd somehow set off inside of her.

But only for a moment. To her great embarrassment, she could feel herself still clenching around his fingers, even after the orgasm was done. Still needing. Still wanting.

Cole cursed low and hard. "You are…you are trying to drive me crazy. You're so wet. I can feel you tugging on my fingers. Begging…"

Sunny didn't realize he was still fully clothed, while she stood there in nothing but her demi bra until he withdrew his hand from her and went to work on getting himself ready for what was to come next. An unzipping noise then one of foil tearing. In a lightening flash he was sheathed, and then he was pushing into her, hard and thick, and way larger than she would have dared to expect.

He pushed and she received him…all the way up to the hilt, moaning with pleasure as she adjusted to his size.

He also bit out a groan, stroking into her as if allowing himself just a few hits—just a few, before he once again went completely still inside of her.

He took a few harsh, unsteady breaths, as if it were taking every ounce of control he had to rein himself in. "Say yes."

"What? Why?" she asked breathless.

"I want to hear you say yes, you want this, you want me."

Obviously she wanted this…him. She'd never been this hot for another man in her entire life. But Sunny's sense of preservation begged her to tell him no again. To gather up her dignity, send him away midcoitus. Then her hips moved again, as if on their own accord, wild and desperate to have him resume moving inside of her.

However, his hands came down in cruel refusal, anchoring her hips to the wall, so that she had no choice but to keep them still. "Say yes. This is nonnegotiable. You lied to me, and you denied me—two of the things that piss me off the most. This is your punishment. Give in. Give in now."

He had to be kidding. He couldn't really expect her to just submit to him like that. But her clit was throbbing against where their bodies met, hot and needy, making it feel as if she would die if he didn't finish what he had started.

"Yes, I want this," she said, getting it out as quickly as she could, so that they could get on with it. "I want you, just please…"

He started moving again in an instant. His body heavy against hers as he filled her up again and again.

"So tight. So wet," he bit out, his voice stretched with anger. "Even better than I thought it would be. And I've been thinking about this a lot. All day."

His hips started banging her hard into the wall with the force of his strokes, as if her quick, quiet words of submission had cut the leash on whatever power of will he was using to hold himself back.

"I hate this," he bit out. "I hate being out of control. I hate how out of control you make me."

But his head came down and he kissed her again, his tongue plunging into her mouth almost as rough and wild as his hard length below. It felt as though he was not just coaxing another orgasm out of her, but demanding it. And that feeling was confirmed when he said, "Too good, too hot. I'm not going to last much longer. Come. Come now, Sunny!"

She came with a long moan, the climax consuming her body in red-hot fire before it finally let her go. Cole came soon after, his cock swelling even thicker inside of her before he released into the condom.

What the hell... Sunny thought to herself, the climax still ringing in her ears and making her feel as disoriented as a bomb victim. *What the hell was that?*

His body pressed hard against hers, his hands still clamped around her hips, his shoulders taut with tension as he emptied out. When he was done, his head fell forward, his forehead coming to rest on the wall, right next to where her own head lay.

She could feel his nose in her hair, his breath hot on her neck as he inhaled then exhaled. Then one of his arms came up and around the back of her neck. And he held her, just held her for what might have been only a few seconds, but it felt like aeons to Sunny's befuddled mind.

He eventually moved away. Pulling out of her with a wet sound as he took a few careful steps back.

Without a word, he took off the condom, his jaw clenching as he disposed of it in a nearby wastebasket. Then he pulled up his pants and pushed himself back inside of them, but not before Sunny took note of the long length of thick flesh between his legs. Still at half-mast.

He went over to the hotel room's closet and got out a robe, which he handed to her, his eyes once again shuttered. Sunny could see that the cold businessman was all the way back in charge now.

And the room, which had been so unbearably hot

just a few minutes ago, became incredibly cold. Shame and embarrassment rushed through her, as if they'd only just been waiting on the sidelines for her to get done demeaning herself, before they started asking her all sorts of judgmental questions. Questions that rang in her ears like fire alarms as she put on the robe.

"I..." She started. "I don't know why I let that happen. We shouldn't have—"

Cole's icy green eyes bored into hers, angry and hard. "You're not going to like what happens next if you finish that sentence."

And the words she'd been about to say died in her throat.

"It happened," he bit out. "And it's going to happen again." He gave her a significant look. "It's definitely going to happen again. The only question now is, what are your terms?"

Chapter 10

"What are my terms?" Sunny repeated carefully as though he were speaking another language.

And Cole was forced to bite back another curse. This is why he preferred to date a certain kind of woman. Women with impressive résumés who didn't make too many demands and were okay with short relationships with no strings attached.

But all he could see were strings when he looked at Sunny, whose curves were not hidden nearly well enough under the hotel robe he'd given her to wear. The Benton's hotel robes were too thin, he decided right then and there. He'd have to talk to someone in Purchasing about ordering better robes. Thick ones that made even the curviest dancer look like a blob and not someone he needed to have again. Right now, on the floor, because the bed was still too far away.

"Yes, your terms," he answered before his lustful thoughts could overtake his reasoning again. "What do you want from me in order to keep this going? Name it."

She gave him a quizzical look. "So what? You're trying to negotiate the terms of a sexual relationship with me? Like I'm some sort of business you want to acquire? Or an escort? Because there are plenty of other women in Las Vegas who will let you do what we just did without—" she hooked her fingers in mocking quotation marks "—terms."

He knew there was. And there were also plenty of women who would let him have anything he wanted from them, without conversation or niceties. But at the moment, he didn't want those women. He only wanted Sunny.

"I'll let you think about it while I go upstairs and put on my tux," he said, heading to the door.

She blinked. "You still want to go to the event?"

"Yes," he said, his hand on the door's handle. "We have to be seen together. Outside of a bedroom if we want Nora to buy our *whirlwind romance*."

"Yeah, but...I kind of don't have a dress to wear now." She cut her eyes to the pile of silk lying ruined on the floor at his feet.

He felt something tick in his jaw just thinking about how out of control he'd been. Barely able to keep himself in check, he'd been so wild to get to her.

"I'll have Agnes send another dress up," he informed her. "Something from one of the boutiques down below."

She crinkled her eyes at him. "That's a pretty easy

solve. Is this like your regular M.O.? Tearing dresses off women and then doing them against the wall?"

He frowned back. Her voice was teasing and light, but he had the feeling she'd just laid out a trap for him. Like she wanted him to say *yes,* he did this all the time, so that she could judge him. Or have an excuse not to let him have her again.

He folded his arms. "Do you want me to say yes, Sunny? Would that make it easier for you?"

Sunny faltered. She obviously hadn't expected to get called out on her tactic. "No, I'm just asking."

"Oh, well, if you're *just asking,*" he said, making sure she could hear the incredulity in his voice before he got into her personal space. He left only an inch of air between them when he bent down close to her ear, "No, you're the only woman I've ever taken like that, the only woman I've ever wanted to take like that. And that's why I'll be expecting your terms by the end of the night."

"And that's why I'll be expecting your terms by the end of the night."

Cole's words rang in her ears all through the uncomfortable ride in the limo to the Businessperson of the Year dinner. Cole was clean-shaven, his hair was slicked back, and he was dressed in a tux that looked as if it had been purposefully designed to hang on his lean frame—or just make it impossible for Sunny not to sneak looks at him across the wide expanse of the limo seat. Looks that accomplished absolutely nothing, because yes, he was still handsome. Even more handsome than before. Every time she looked. Every single time.

She was once again dressed in an evening gown, but this one was a bit more daring. Red with a plunging neckline and a slit that ran nearly up to her thigh. She'd been surprised when it had been delivered to her hotel room door. It wasn't at all like anything she'd imagine Agnes choosing.

And she'd been right to be surprised. Cole's eyes had roamed over her with cool inspection when she'd arrived in the lobby. "I was right. That dress does suit you better," he had told her.

So now he was picking out her clothes as well as trying to shark her into bed with his demands that she name her terms, as though she were some business deal he was looking to close.

If *The Benton Girls* wasn't counting on her, and if Nora hadn't called her up earlier that evening, delighted that Cole was bringing her as his date to tonight's event, she probably would have backed out of the deal entirely. She really didn't need this grief. Really, really didn't need it...

She snuck another look at Cole, only to have her eyes get tangled with his when he caught her. "Like what you see?" he asked, his arrogant face cool with amusement.

"No..." Then, she said, "Actually, yes," because it seemed too childish to deny what she'd been caught doing. "But it really doesn't matter. You're hot. Really freaking handsome. So what? I'm sure you get told that all the time."

He raised his eyebrows. "Do you always sound so unhappy when you give out compliments?"

"No, I'm a great compliment giver. It usually makes me happy to give credit where credit is due."

"But not in <u>this</u> case," he said, his voice tinged with triumph as if he were handily winning the argument.

Sunny sighed and turned to look out the window at the bright lights of the Vegas strip flying by. "Do you always make it this hard for people to give you compliments and be done with it?"

She could feel his smirking eyes on the back of her head. "Am I making your life harder, Sunny?"

"I think you know exactly what you're doing." Sunny answered as they pulled up to the hotel where the dinner was being held.

Relief flooded her at the thought of no longer having to share a small and intimate space with Cole.

But the feeling didn't last long. Tomas, who'd been introduced to her earlier as Cole's regular driver and for work and special events, let Cole out first. And though Tomas opened the door for her, too, it was Cole who held his hand out to her when it came time to climb out of the long black car.

She placed her hand in his, feeling the exact same as she would if a bear had offered her his paw. Like it was a very dangerous invitation to take.

He's just acting, he's just acting, she told herself, as she stood listening to a conversation Cole was having with a fellow hotel magnate, who'd wanted to know more about Cole's plans to expand the Benton brand into more mid-range hotels.

Their conversation was actually pretty interesting. Sunny hadn't known Cole had such big plans. No wonder he worked all the time. But she felt a little weird just standing there, while Cole did all the talking. It made her feel like a trophy—in fact, she wondered if this was how trophy girlfriends often felt, as if they were on display, just there to be looked at by all the other men at the party.

However, Sunny wasn't sure if they were looking because she was Cole's date or because she definitely didn't look like any of the other trophy wives or girl-friends. Mostly blondes, cool and elegant, who looked as though they'd been born in black evening gowns with perfectly coiffed hair and understated makeup. She'd gotten several looks from the other women at the party already, and they didn't even try to disguise exactly what they were thinking: "What are *you* doing here?"

The whole situation made Sunny want to slink back outside and wait in the limo until Cole was done. How-ever, Cole hadn't let go of her hand since they'd gotten out of the limo. In fact, he'd kept her by his side the entire cocktail hour, not even letting go when other businesspeople came over to congratulate him and shake his hand. For what? A business deal? She still wasn't quite sure.

"Occupied," he'd said with a rueful smile, before introducing her as, "My date, Sunny Johnson."

It made her feel like his possession. Yet, it also made her feel safe, as if she didn't have to worry about getting eaten alive by the other sharks at the party, be-cause he was holding on to her tight. Instead of aban-doning her, he'd chosen to keep her by his side all night. So it also kind of made her feel special.

And that was why she had to keep reminding her-self that he was just acting. That he was putting on a show for his grandmother. Nora had greeted them enthusiastically when they came in and then spent the rest of the cocktail hour throwing several approving glances their way, even while she was mingling with other attendees.

Sunny found out that Cole was actually left-handed at dinner when he proceeded to eat his entire meal with one hand while talking to the vice president of a neighboring hotel. Luckily Sunny was right-handed and she was also happy that she'd been seated with Nora on her other side.

Since Nora's other grandson, Max, had yet to show up, Nora spent most of the dinner chatting with her. Cole had been right about one thing, the prospect of them getting together had certainly made his grandmother happy.

"I knew you two would be the perfect match! I knew it!" she said at one point.

Yet another cool blonde walked past their table. She gave Sunny a hostile stare, even as she said, "Lovely event, Nora. Congratulations."

"Thank you, dearie," Nora answered, her own eyes cooling as they watched the thin blonde move away.

"Wow, that was like a really polite drive-by," Sunny said.

"Oh, don't mind her," Nora said, her eyes warming right back up again when she turned back to Sunny. They were the exact same green as Cole's, but Sunny couldn't imagine his eyes ever possessing such warmth, especially when looking at her.

"Her and all those other girls have been after Cole for years, and he's never given any one of them more than a month or two of his time. He shows up here with you, clearly taken by you, and of course, they're going to get their knickers in a bunch, wondering what it is you have that they don't. It was the same for me when Cole's grandfather started bringing me around to these functions. The showgirls are supposed to stay on the stage kicking up their legs. We're not supposed to ever come down to mix it up with the ones making the money off our gams."

Nora's face darkened with remembered bitterness. "The younger ones accept me now, because I've been around long enough and I raise lots of money for my different charities. But the older ones still look at me like I don't belong. Like I'll never be good enough."

This statement made Sunny feel for Nora— especially in light of her poor health. But it also confused her. "They didn't accept you, but you're happy Cole's ah...*taken with*...someone who doesn't quite fit in either?"

Nora graced another blonde passerby with a beneficent smile that totally belied her next words, "Dearie, I'd hang myself with me own rope if Cole married any of these old money witches. I deserve a good granddaughter—one I can talk to just as easily as my old friend, Berta."

Now she took Sunny's other hand and squeezed it, her face fond with memories of Sunny's grandmother. "I missed her so much when Cole's grandfather pulled me off *The Revue* line and into his world, but she always seemed to know when I truly needed her. I'd start to feel down about not fitting in, and there'd be Berta, ringing me up, inviting me over to the apartment we used to share for dinner, or insisting we go out for a few drinks. That was before you young ones came up with the phrase *Girls' Night Out*, but Berta always seemed to know when I needed one. I'll never forgive myself for falling out of touch with her after that no-good son of mine was born…"

Nora's eyes became watery with regret for a moment. She recovered quickly, though, pasting a smile on her face and patting Sunny's hand. "But then you joined *The Revue* and you're such a lovely soul, Sunny, just like your gran. It's like I have a second chance now, and seeing you with Cole does my heart a world of good. So thank you for taking him on, dearie. I know he can be quite challenging, but so was his grandda. The man would have worked himself into an early grave if I hadn't come along to distract him, and I just want my Cole to be happy, truly happy like his grandda was."

Sunny felt her own eyes brimming with tears. And if she still had any doubts about Cole's plan to ease Nora's mind in the last months of her life, they disappeared.

She squeezed Nora's hand back, and said, "You're right. Who cares what anyone else thinks? Your approval is all I need."

"That's right!" Nora told her. "The rest of them can kiss our Irish behinds!"

Sunny laughed. "But I'm not Irish, Nora."

"I'm giving you honorary citizenship," Nora informed her. "'Cos I'm rich, and I can do whatever I want."

Sunny's reply of laughter was interrupted by a musical swell, and then all conversation came to an end as all eyes turned toward the stage, where an older man in a tux came to stand behind the podium.

After a few opening jokes, he said, "I was honored to receive this award last year, after 35 years in

Las Vegas, and even though tonight's award winner won't be able to enjoy AARP membership for at least 20 years, I fully approve of the board's choice. This young man has drive and has done more for his family's business holdings in ten years than I've done in 35. I couldn't be more honored to present this year's Businessperson of the Year award to Cole Benton, CEO of the Benton Holdings."

Polite applause sounded and Sunny turned to Cole with wide eyes. "Wait, *you're* the Businessperson of the Year? Oh, my gosh, congratulations! Why didn't you tell me?"

She felt slightly guilty, thinking of how she'd tried to get out of coming here with him earlier. She would have not only stranded him without a date, but she also would have diminished the experience for his grandmother, who might not have many more chances to see her grandson receive awards like this one.

Cole just smirked and gave her a peck on her surprised mouth before standing up and finally letting go of her hand.

His speech was short and to the point. An almost terse list of milestones The Benton Group had reached under his leadership and an only slightly less terse list of what he had planned for the corporation's future.

Sunny could tell he wasn't even trying to amuse the crowd as the man who'd introduced him had. In fact, if his body language was any indicator, he thought all this pomp and circumstance was silly, and he'd much rather be in his office, making The Benton Group as great as his vision for it, rather than giving all these overstuffed businesspeople a bullet list.

Sunny's heart swelled with happiness for him, anyway. This was a special night for both Cole and his grandmother, and she was very proud of him.

But then his stance softened a bit, and instead of irritated, he seemed slightly uncomfortable as he said, "But before I go, I'd like to thank one person in particular..."

To Sunny's surprise, his eyes landed on her. "Sunny Johnson, we've only known each other a short time, but you've made my life brighter. This award means more to me because you're by my side. Thank you."

Sunny didn't realize her heart had stopped beating for a few moments while he spoke, until it came back with a thunderous roar. His sentiment was easily the nicest thing any man had ever said about her in public. And even though she knew it was just Cole acting a part, she couldn't help but be touched.

Nora also seemed moved by Cole's unexpected words of gratitude toward Sunny. "He really seems truly smitten with you," she said, her eyes full of wonder. Like Sunny was some kind of miracle worker. "It's just like when his grandda and me met. Oh, we knew. Right away we did."

"Excuse me," Sunny said, standing up.

She hated to be so abrupt with Nora, but she suddenly felt overwhelmed with emotion. Cole had no idea what she'd been through with Derek, or how his words, no matter how fake, would affect her. She rushed to the bathroom, needing a moment to compose herself before she could face Cole and play her part again.

Luckily the restroom was empty. She braced herself against the marble sink, letting the cool surface seep into her hands. She breathed and reminded herself, "It's just an act. It's just an act..." until the tears backed down and she could feel her emotions leveling out.

She gave herself five more minutes, wishing she could splash her face with a little cool water before she went back out there, but it would be hard to play her part make-up free.

Instead, she reached into her purse and applied another smear of lipstick across her full mouth.

Mask back on, she opened the door to face Cole and return to being the new love of his life—only to run straight into someone's chest. Someone's very muscular chest.

"Oh, no..." she said, her face full of apologies as she looked up, way up, at one of the most handsome men she'd ever seen.

Even if she hadn't met Max at Nora's Christmas event, she would have recognized him as Cole's brother. His features were also chiseled, but in a way that brought to mind a Greek statue as opposed to a predatory bird. The only thing that kept him from being too pretty was the slightly askew angle of his nose, a ridged testament to a long-ago break that didn't properly set. His hair was also much darker than Cole's, black and silky, but his eyes were the same light green.

However, whereas Cole's eyes were piercing, Max's had a playfully wicked gleam in them that Sunny suspected just might be permanent.

"Hi, again, Max," Sunny said, then she grimaced at the brown smudge on his formerly crisp white tuxedo shirt. "Sorry for getting makeup on your shirt."

"So it's true, you're here with my brother," he said

with a shake of his head. "Just goes to prove what Grandpa used to say, 'Nora always gets her way.'"

"Ah, well…" Sunny didn't know how she felt about not only lying to Nora about the nature of her relationship with Cole, but also to his brother. "I'm just glad we could make her happy."

She reached into her clutch and pulled out a makeup remover wipe. "Here, let me get that," she said, wiping her makeup off his shirt.

"Wow, that actually worked," he said, when she finished, and his shirt was once again white.

"These wipes are like magic. I can't tell you how many times they've saved me from a costume change." She gave him an embarrassed smile. "I can be kind of clumsy sometimes."

He smiled back at her, his own eyes twinkling, "You're pretty charming, sweetheart. I can see why my brother decided to roll over for Nora in this case. But poor me, I would've flown back from Italy sooner if I'd known Cole would beat me to the punch."

Sunny's nose wrinkled. There was something weird about how he talked about her and Cole's relationship, almost as if he knew it was fake. However, instead of being grateful that they were honoring Nora's last wishes, he seemed amused, like this was all some sort of game.

"What do you mean by Cole beat you to the punch?" she asked.

Chapter 11

Cole didn't like this situation. He didn't like it at all. First what happened in the hotel room. He'd gone there, planning to tell Sunny in the most businesslike way possible that she was to immediately come back to his penthouse, but instead he'd ended up taking her against the wall. Like an animal, who had no control over himself.

If there was one thing Cole hated, it was feeling out of control. You didn't make it to Businessperson of the Year in less than fifteen years by not having control over yourself. Cole had worked like a fiend to get himself to where he was today, and he didn't appreciate this showgirl coming along, distracting him, not only from his work, but also the bigger plan.

Sunny had been right about one thing. This was only supposed to be a business arrangement, something designed to prevent his grandmother from doing something crazy before he could get her kicked off the board and remove the threat of his good-for-nothing brother getting control of the business.

So why then was he giving more mental energy to Sunny, thinking about having her again and again until he got his fill, than he was to his business? And why couldn't he stop himself from behaving like a lunatic when it came to her?

He'd meant to let go of her hand as soon as they got to the event. Let her keep his grandmother distracted during the business dinner while he talked shop with the only people who mattered in his world, other powerful businesspeople. But when he'd walked in with Sunny, he'd seen the surprise on his fellow businesspeople's faces. That he didn't mind. He knew that they were an unconventional couple—even by Vegas standards.

What he minded were the looks that had followed the surprise. Heated looks that let Cole know he wasn't the only one affected by Sunny's combination of curves and good looks. He wasn't the only one who'd be more than willing to ravage her behind closed doors.

And suddenly he'd found himself unwilling to let go of her hand, to the point that he barely let other men talk to her beyond a short introduction. Then he'd taken over all conversation from there, his voice level, but his eyes sending the "don't touch, she's mine" message loud and clear. He'd actually considered bringing her up onstage with him, so everyone in the room would know who she'd come here with, and who would be taking her home tonight.

What the hell was wrong with him?

And that last part of his speech. Tacked on at the end, meant to sell the story he was peddling to Nora. But like an actor who took his craft too seriously, he'd found himself actually believing the lies he was spewing. For a moment there, the stupid award that hadn't meant much to him beyond an obligation to attend a function that would take him away from his work, actually did mean something. And it was because Sunny was out there in the audience, her open face clearly conveying how proud she was of him.

"You're clearly infatuated," Nora said under her breath when she made her way up to him through the sea of people rushing to congratulate him and shake his now free hand after the speech. "Didn't I tell you she was special?"

"That you did," he answered, his eyes searching the room for Sunny.

"She's in the powder room," Nora informed him, "so you can give your dear old gran some of your precious attention while you're waiting for her to come out."

He returned his attention to Nora. "Sorry, Nora, I wasn't aware attention was what you wanted from me," he said, his voice tight.

He didn't appreciate being manipulated by her, or having his hand forced, and it was hard for him to keep his resentment on a leash while talking with her.

But if she noticed, he couldn't tell past the smug and triumphant look on her face. "All I'm really wanting from you, dear grandson, is a 'you were right and I was wrong, sweet Gran.'"

It would be a cold day in hell before Cole said that,

but he was saved from having to tell her so when he saw Sunny emerge from the restroom—only to run into his brother, Max.

He watched Max smile down at her, his head tilted in the way Cole recognized as full-on flirting. Then Sunny pulled out some kind of cloth and started wiping the front of his shirt. Touching him. *She was touching him.*

Cole's blood ran cold and he abandoned his grandmother without a word of explanation.

"Cole, where are you going?" he heard her ask behind him.

"What do you mean Cole beat you to the punch?" Sunny repeated.

Max Benton looked back at her, the expression on his face quizzical. "Wait, Cole didn't tell you about Nora?"

She answered him with an equally quizzical look of her own. "Yeah, of course he told me Nora is sick, but what does that have to do with him beating you to the punch?"

Max paused, the gleam in his eyes going from wicked to shrewd as he opened his mouth to say something else—only to have Cole swoop in from out of nowhere.

"There you are, Sunny," he said, threading his fingers through hers, with a smile that didn't get anywhere close to his eyes. He turned to his brother. "Max, you're just now getting here? You missed my speech."

Max grinned, and he seemed to quite deliberately let his own green gaze linger on Sunny for a few more moments before raising it to look at Cole. "Missed the speech, but it looks like I got here right on time for the show. You two are putting on quite an act for Nora. Poor, sick, Nora." His wicked eyes lingered on Cole.

Sunny sensed something frost over in Cole, even though his expression was still set on neutral. "Actually, you're too late for that, too. Sunny and I were just leaving."

Sunny raised her eyebrows at him. They were?

Max frowned big with mock disappointment. "Already? But I just got here. And I'm sure you've been boring poor Sunny to death all night." He gave Sunny a pitying look. "Cole lives in Vegas but never learned to play. Not even a little bit." He pulled out a card and held it out to her. "But if you're ever interested in having some fun, call me."

Even if Sunny had been thinking to reach for the card, she wouldn't have had a chance. All the civility fell away from Cole's face, and as his hand gripped hers tighter as he stepped to Max, blocking Sunny's view of him and his proffered business card.

"Why do you have a business card, Max?" she heard him ask. "It's not like you do any real work for our company. Also, maybe you haven't noticed yet, but Sunny's here with me."

"But is she having a good time?" she heard Max respond. "That's all I was trying to find out."

Cole's shoulders flexed angrily underneath his tux, and for a few seconds, Sunny was afraid he was going to punch his own brother right there in front of his grandmother and everyone else.

But at the last moment, Cole stepped back and walked away from Max without another word. Pulling Sunny along with him across the room, and right out of the party. He didn't even stop to say goodbye to Nora.

The next thing Sunny knew, they were back in the limo. Cole finally let go of her hand just as the car pulled away from the curb.

"Um…do you want to talk about that?" she asked him.

He reached into his tux and took out his smartphone. "Not particularly," he answered, without looking up from his phone. His were thumbs flying over its keyboard graphic.

Sunny clamped her lips in irritation before rephrasing. "Okay, Cole, I'm not asking. I'm telling you we need to talk about what just happened in there."

Cole kept on typing.

"What are you doing that's so important you can't have a conversation about pulling me out of that party, like I was your toy and you were taking me home?"

"I'm emailing my lawyer about an addendum to the contract you signed," he answered. "You'll need to agree not to communicate or be seen with Max."

"Are you kidding me?" Sunny asked him, her brain near exploding with outrage.

"I never kid about business," Cole said. "And Max is bad for business. Irresponsible. Useless. He's never done anything for the company except tarnish our image tomcatting all over the world. I don't want him bothering you."

Sunny, who'd never had a sibling, but had often wished for one growing up, found his attitude toward his brother alarming. "Really? He didn't seem that bad. A little flirty, but nothing I couldn't handle. We don't have to add an addendum to what was only supposed to be a confidentiality agreement."

He looked up from his typing, his face hard. "I think we do."

"I'm telling you we don't, Cole. Nora was really happy tonight. Really happy. I'm doing this for her. And I'm not looking to disappoint her in any way. I'm happy to stay far away from Max, especially if he doesn't have her best interest at heart."

Cole's shoulders relaxed, but only a little. He let a few seconds of silence go by then said, "I like to be in control."

"I'm getting that," Sunny answered, her voice laced with wry amusement.

"No, you're not," he bit out. "If you got that, we wouldn't even be having this conversation, because you wouldn't have been flirting with Max right in front of me. *Touching him...*"

"I got makeup on his shirt! I was trying to wipe it off! What is wrong with you? We're just supposed to be pretending we're together. Why are you being so crazy? It's just pretend—"

He was across the seat before she could fully finish her declaration, mauling her with his mouth, his tongue taking total possession.

She should have pushed him away, screamed at him to get off of her, because he was acting like a maniac. But she didn't. Instead, she kissed him back, desperate for his mouth.

Her brain went into a complete short-circuit, and for minutes on end, nothing else registered except the feel of his lips, and the press of his body against hers. But even his hot kiss became not enough for her after a while. She wanted him. All of him. And even though she was still a bit tender from their earlier session in the hotel room, she started thinking about ripping her own dress off if it would get him where she wanted him to be that much faster.

But then he broke off with a curse, tearing his lips from hers.

He sat up and he looked as if he was expending his entire reserve of willpower as he sat back down in his own seat, moving as far away from her as possible.

"Wha… Why…?" Sunny could barely form a coherent thought after their kiss. But she wanted to know, why had he stopped? Why?

Maybe he could read her mind, because he then said, "I don't have a condom." His eyes focused on his window as if he couldn't even bear to look at her in that moment.

"Oh…" Sunny said, her voice small, and she sat up straight in her seat, tugging up the dress's sweetheart bodice, when she realized it was down past her nipples, her breasts nearly entirely exposed.

"Oh," was all she said. She had no words left, none that could possibly explain why she melted like a stick of butter whenever he turned up the heat.

The rest of the ride passed by in silence. Sunny was surprised when he spoke again, right after the car stopped in the hotel garage.

"Are you on birth control?" he asked her, his voice a complete monotone.

Sunny opened her mouth.

"Just nod yes or no, Sunny. I'm not in the mood for questions."

Sunny nodded.

He put his hand on the door's latch. "You can stay in the hotel room tonight, but tomorrow I'll be kicking you out. You won't have access to that hotel room, or any other Benton room in the city. I'll have Agnes arrange for you to get the necessary blood tests tomorrow. We'll both prove we're clean, and then…"

Finally he turned to look at her. "And then you'll come to me, Sunny. I don't care what you agreed to before. You can name your terms and I'll meet them, but for the rest of the summer you'll share my bed. This is how it's going to be between us."

"And what if I…" Sunny swallowed, trying not to react to the way her core tightened at the thought of spending the rest of summer in his bed. "And what if I say no?"

His green eyes turned to her, and Sunny could have sworn they'd turned a few shades darker in the shadow of the back seat.

"You won't like what I do if you say no," he answered, his voice cold.

So cold, Sunny felt frozen to the spot.

He let himself out of the limo, leaving her there in the backseat without another word.

Chapter 12

"You won't like what I do if you say no."

The words still echoed in Sunny's head, even though it had been over twelve hours since she had first heard them. Just like they'd repeated in her head while she was packing her large suitcase for the third time in just a few days and when she was driving back to her apartment in the four-door Mercedes Cole had lent her for the summer.

What other choice did she have, but to return to her own place? She wasn't a blow-up doll that Cole Benton got to decide when and where to use. She had her own will. And dignity! Of course she'd gone back to her own apartment. And she planned to stay there for the rest of the summer.

In fact, if Cole came at her again with his outrageous demands, she planned to ask for an addendum of her own. No more time spent alone. The public dates she'd agreed to go on with him would take place entirely in public. No more intimate limo rides. They'd meet each other at the venue and leave in separate cars. No more kisses, and definitely no more hanky panky. She was done getting bullied by Cole Benton.

So why couldn't she stop thinking about him? The way he'd kissed her, the feel of his hands on her hips as he drove into her against the wall—even the way his eyes had darkened in the limo right before he'd given her his ultimatum.

Why couldn't she get him out of her mind no matter what she did?

Her phone had rung less than five minutes after the official checkout time on Monday, the screen lighting up with Agnes's name. Sunny sent it straight to voice mail, ignoring the ping and the tape icon that appeared on her screen a few seconds later.

A few minutes later the phone went off again. This time from a Las Vegas number she didn't know. She also let that call go to voice mail. But this time when the message icon appeared, she pushed Play.

"Sunny, this is Cole—"

She immediately pushed the delete option, knowing on instinct that she did not want to hear what he'd say after his curt introduction.

The phone started ringing again fifteen minutes later. Sunny sent it straight to voice mail, only to have her phone go off again after another fifteen minutes.

Sunny sent a text to both the phone number and the email address Cole had given her. If there's a public event you'd like me to attend before our scheduled dinner at The Benton Golf Club on Tuesday, have Agnes email me.

She then pushed Send. And shortly after her phone lit up with yet another call from Cole. Sunny decided this would be a good time to just turn off her phone altogether.

Sunny looked at her wall clock. It was only 11:30 a.m. How could time pass by so slow?

By twelve, she was beside herself with boredom and anxiety. Unable to focus on any task for too long or even to sit down for more than a few minutes at a time.

Remembering what Nora had said about how much she regretted losing touch with Sunny's grandmother, she turned on her phone and swiped past all the missed calls and voice mail notifications to ring up Pru.

"Hey, girl, I was just thinking about you!" Pru said, when she answered the phone. "Wondering if we were still going to do our Monday Mani now that you're working for Nora Benton."

"Of course we are," Sunny answered with a laugh, happy that Pru hadn't planned to treat her any differently now that they were no longer on the line together. They'd made a tradition of going in for "upkeep" every other week together. Stage dancers required what Sunny jokingly referred to as "regular maintenance." And Rick was one to check. She'd seen him call out a dancer for leg stubble, although how he could have possibly known, considering she was wearing tights. A mystery still whispered about by dancers every week as they got their manis, pedis, and waxing done.

An idea occurred to her. "Do you have anything planned for right after?" she asked Pru.

"Nope. Just vegging out in front of the TV until it's time to pick up Jakey," Pru answered.

"Then how about we get massages, too? My treat."

"Really? Oh, man, I could use one. I chaperoned a hike yesterday for Jake's nature club, and all that walking. My back is killing me. But I wouldn't want to put you out."

"It wouldn't be putting me out," Sunny assured her. "And believe me, I could use a massage, too."

It was true, though not for nearly as wholesome reasons. As it turned out, her session against the wall with Cole had worked out a few muscles she was no longer used to using.

"But I wouldn't want to make you pay. I know you're still saving up for New York."

Guilt warmed Sunny's cheeks. She wasn't used to keeping things from Pru, but she'd signed a confidentiality agreement. However, she also really wanted a massage, and she knew Pru wouldn't spend the money on herself. She put every extra penny she had into her younger brother, paying expensive rent on a one-bedroom in a neighborhood with a good high school, also keeping him in braces and a constant stream of things needed in order for him to play soccer after school. "You'd think it'd be cheap. It's just kicking a ball around, right? But his team tells me like every other week, I've gotta pay this and that so Jake can kick the ball around with his friends. And so here am I, forking over all this money, even though I don't even like soccer— The things I do for that kid…"

It was true, and Sunny knew for a fact that Pru wouldn't do something special for herself if Sunny didn't both pay for it and insist she take it as a gift.

"I've budgeted it all out," she told Pru. "And I've got enough left over for a couple of massages. Don't worry."

"How much is this new job as Nora Benton's assistant paying you? And does she need a replacement when you leave town? Because Jakey's got to be put through college, and I won't be able to make a living kicking up my heels forever, you know."

Sunny did *know*. And she worried about how Pru would survive after she aged out of dancing. Yet another thing to feel guilty about as she lied, "The compensation's pretty good, but it's a temporary gig. I'll be leaving in August for sure. So we only have a limited amount of girl time left. Please say you'll come get a massage with me."

"I don't know."

"Please, Pru. I don't want to go alone!"

Pru laughed. "Fine, fine. I'll come with you, but we'll have to go to the spa at The Benton. That way at least I can pitch in by letting you use my employee discount."

"Ah…" Sunny racked her brain, trying to come up with a plausible excuse for why they shouldn't get their massages at The Benton—the hotel she'd just vowed never to step foot in again. Yesterday.

But there was no way to explain to Pru that Cole Benton did something to her that made her lose all sense of herself—really all sense of anything. Or how she didn't trust herself to even be in the same building as him at this point.

There was no way to explain that at all. Not without breaking her confidentiality agreement. So Sunny caved. "Okay, we can do it at The Benton. But can you meet me there sooner than later? Like in a half an hour?"

"Sure!" Pru answered.

Her easy answer caused Sunny to let out a small breath of relief. She didn't want to be anywhere near The Benton when Cole got off of work.

It only took five minutes into her side-by-side massage with Pru for Sunny to stop regretting her decision to come.

"I'm sorry, girl," she told Pru, who was lying facedown on a table nearby. "You used to be my best friend, but now Helga is."

Helga chuckled softly and said, "I am glad you are enjoying it."

Sometimes more upscale spas had a limited color selection for manicures, but The Benton Spa wasn't one of them. Pru chose a tasteful beige—that being one of the few colors Rick accepted on the line.

But Sunny wasn't on the line anymore, so she snatched up a bright yellow, one she knew would pop against her skin tone and go well with nearly everything in her wardrobe.

"Ooh, look at you," Pru said, when the technician started applying the second layer of yellow to her toes. Then she pulled out her camera phone and took a snapshot. "I'm sending this to Rick."

A few seconds later, the phone dinged with Rick's reply and Pru laughed. "He says you're lucky you're not on the line anymore!"

"Yeah, lucky…." Sunny let out a weak laugh. She was really starting to regret signing that confidentiality agreement. She wished she could confide in Pru, let her know how bored she was with nothing to really do but twiddle her thumbs all day and how she wished she could rejoin *The Revue.* At least then she'd have something to occupy her mind.

Something other than Cole Benton.

"Ooh, as long as you're doing something new today, you should go ahead and get the fully baldy when we go in for our wax," Pru advised. "Really give that new boyfriend of yours a treat."

Sunny's mouth dropped open. "What? How did you…?"

"Girl, did you really think you could go to an event with Cole Benton, get your picture snapped all over the place, and Rick wouldn't send all of us the dirt, like it was the company newsletter?"

Sunny's stomach sank. She hadn't taken that into account. So it was actually happening. Her fake relationship with Cole was public now, and soon everybody that she knew would think she was seriously dating Cole Benton.

"All I have to say is good for you. You've been letting your breakup with Derek mess with your head for too long. It's about time you got out there again. That Cole Benton cleans up nice, and the way he was looking at you in those pictures—like he wanted to eat you up. So tonight, let him!"

The lady working on her toes looked up. "If you'd like I can change your requested service order. We give all the first timers to Marsha. She's the best when it comes to full waxes. Very gentle." She winked at Sunny. "But you have to wait at least twenty-four hours to have sex after getting it done."

"Um…" Sunny said.

"So tomorrow night, *let him!*" Pru revised with a laugh. "Yeah, she definitely wants to go with the full baldy. A couple of the girls on the line say their boyfriends love it."

Sunny could not have blushed harder if an industrial heat lamp had been turned on her.

Sunny ended up walking a little funny when she went to the front desk to pay for their services. Not because it had hurt too much—the technician had been as capable as claimed and gentle to the touch. But because she wasn't used to being bare down below.

"I don't understand why women do that to themselves," Derek had complained the one time she'd mentioned going with Pru to get a simple bikini wax. "You're all victims of Big Cosmetics' agenda," he scoffed.

However, Sunny liked the feel of nothing between her skin and her underwear as she walked. It was curiously tantalizing in a way that would've had her thoughts turning to Cole Benton if she hadn't promised herself she wouldn't think about him in that capacity any longer. And she hadn't, except during the conversation with Pru, and during the massage, and okay, every time her mind wasn't actively engaged in thinking about something else.

But other than those errant thoughts, the spa afternoon had been exactly what Sunny needed, rejuvenating, relaxing, and most of all, distracting.

She was more than happy to hand over her credit card to the attendant at the front desk.

But the attendant shook her head with a gentle smile. "Oh, no, Ms. Johnson. There's no charge for today."

Pru grinned and elbowed her in the side. "Ooh, it looks like somebody hooked you up."

Sunny did not return her smile. "Of course there's a charge," she insisted to the attendant. "The service was excellent and I want everyone to get paid, with a tip."

"I assure you they will all be compensated," the attendant answered.

"But how about the tip?"

"Please don't worry about that, Ms. Johnson. It's all been taken care of."

"By who?" Sunny asked, though she could already guess. "Because I'm really not comfortable with anyone else paying my bills. Even if he is the head of this hotel. So if you could just put the balance on this card."

The woman lowered her eyes. "I really can't take that from you. I have my orders," she said like she was merely a soldier and the general had spoken.

With a suck of her teeth, Sunny made the decision to put her card back in her clutch. Not because she wanted Cole to exert this kind of control over her, even when he wasn't present, but because she sensed she would be making this woman's job much harder if she insisted on paying for it herself.

"Fine," Sunny said. "But whatever tip you're giving them, could you up it to fifty percent of the service? I'd be happy to put that on my card if it's too much for *whoever's* taking care of it."

The woman held up a finger and moved away to have a whispered conversation with her manager, who then picked up the house phone. After a short conversation with whoever was on the other like, he nodded at the attendant, who came back to the still unused register, her eyes delighted. "No, it's not. Whatever you want in any Benton hotel, it's all taken care of, Ms. Johnson."

"Wow!" Pru said beside her. "Does your guy have any friends who are dying to take on a woman with a brother-slash-ward?"

Sunny turned to her with a pasted-on smile and said, "How about if we go have some lunch, go see a movie, and then later on I can take you and Jakey out to dinner with the money I saved on our spa day?"

Pru shook her head. "Oh, I was just kidding, you don't have to—"

"I insist," Sunny said, pulling her friend away from the counter, and toward the door quickly. Very quickly. She had a feeling Cole Benton was already headed down there in his private elevator. "Lunch and dinner. Anywhere you like—as long as it's not a Benton Group holding."

Dinner at the Olive Garden was great and Sunny even managed to stretch it out to a little bit of TV afterward on Pru's couch while Jakey did his homework at the table. The girlfriend time was terrific and long overdue, but when Jakey yawned and asked Sunny if she was planning on sleeping over, Sunny took that as her cue to get out of her friend's hair and thanked her for putting up with her for nearly the entire day.

"No, thank *you,* honey," Pru insisted with a warm hug at her front door. "You know I don't get out much, and that was seriously the best time I've had in a while."

Sunny began to say something else, about how maybe it wouldn't be so bad if Pru started dating again. Jakey was nearly seventeen, and he was mature and kind. Sunny was sure he wouldn't be upset if his pretty sister resumed the life she'd been living before she took over his care.

But before she could say anything, Jakey called out to her that the water wasn't warming up in his shower.

Pru rolled her eyes. "I keep telling the landlord he needs to send someone over to look at our water heater, but he figures as long as the water gets lukewarm most of the time, it's not anything he has to fix. I'll see you in two weeks, girl."

Sunny was left alone again with nothing but the car Cole Benton had insisted she drive around town and a phone she didn't dare to turn back on.

But at least she'd made it through another day without any contact with Cole. Or another appearance from the rat who'd stolen her protein bar. So she congratulated herself as she got out of the Mercedes and headed to her apartment.

Only to stop short when she found Cole Benton waiting outside her apartment door!

Chapter 13

Cole had almost given up on Sunny returning to her apartment. The Mercedes hadn't been there when he arrived at her door, and he'd had no idea if she'd decided to stay there or with the friend she'd come to the salon with—Prudence Washington, who apparently was also a Benton Girl.

But just as he'd been about to call Agnes and tell her to dredge up this Prudence Washington's address, Sunny pulled up in his car. Then climbed out with a satisfied little smile on her face, like she'd gotten away with something.

But that smile fell away as soon as she saw him... and what he was standing next to.

"Is that? Is that an eviction notice?" she nearly screeched, looking at the neon-colored piece of paper posted on her door.

"Name your terms, Sunny," he said between gritted teeth.

"How did you…?" She went to the door and tugged on the large lock that now resided around its knob. "And you locked me out, too? I've never missed a rent check in my life. This is so illegal."

Cole shrugged, liking that she was the one now miserable because of something he'd done, as opposed to vice versa.

"I told you I didn't want you living here."

"Yeah, and so what?" Sunny answered. "I'm a grown woman, Cole, I can do what I want. You don't own me."

"Maybe not, but I own this building."

"What!"

"I put in an offer. The owner took it. He's evicting you."

"What? You can't do that! There are tenant laws. And besides, who does that? Who goes and buys someone's building just so I can't live in it?"

Cole had been asking himself the same thing all morning, as he'd set the deal up, but he kept his tone set on bored when he answered, "Regardless. That's the situation. And you might be right about the tenant laws, but it's going to take you a while to get a court date."

Sunny stared at him for a few hot seconds, and then she started back toward the car.

"Where are you going?" he demanded.

She didn't answer, just kept on walking.

"Don't make me buy your friend Prudence's building, too," he called after her. "She has a brother who needs to be in that district, I hear, and she can't afford to fight me in court when she gets her eviction notice."

That brought Sunny up short, and she turned around with a fierce glare. God, she was beautiful angry. Cole had never seen anything like it.

"You wouldn't," she said.

"I told you last night that you wouldn't like what I did if you said no," he answered. "Now unless you want me to buy Prudence's building, too, you'll stop this and—"

She didn't let him finish. "And what?" she asked. "Submit? Is that what you want? To own me like I'm one of your cars?"

He removed the space between them in just two strides and grabbed onto her arm. "You know what I want, and you want it, too. You're the one playing crazy games with my head. Responding to me the way you did, then disappearing when I asked you to share my bed."

"You didn't ask me, you commanded me. Like a complete psycho. And now you're evicting me and threatening my friend. How did you expect this to go? Do women usually respond to these tactics?"

"I don't know, Sunny," he answered coldly. "You're the only woman I've ever had to manipulate back into my bed. You seem bent on not only denying me but also denying yourself. Why is that?"

"I don't know," she answered, bulging her eyes out at him. "Maybe because you're a psycho?"

Cole didn't love being called a psycho by the woman he wanted in his bed, but this time he didn't take the bait. "A psycho you said you wanted last night in that hotel room. And what was that you said in the limo about me being 'really freaking handsome'?"

To his great satisfaction, the self-righteous indignation drained out of her face and was replaced by a series of flustered expressions before she spluttered, "Last night was a *mistake*. One of the worst mistakes I've ever made. I tried to tell you it was a *mistake* then, but you wouldn't let me."

Her words hit him like an arrow through the heart, lethal and unexpected. And for a moment, just a moment, he let his guard down. But a moment was all it took.

Her eyes widened as her expression went from annoyed to concerned. "Cole? Cole, are you all right?"

He turned away from her, giving her his back.

"Cole?" he heard her say behind him.

He didn't answer her. Couldn't answer her. *Breathe. Don't act. Don't speak until you've got yourself under control,* he told himself.

He hadn't had to give himself this particular instruction in a while. Years. But there was something about Sunny, something that made the self-control he'd started taking for granted a real struggle.

She was right. This had been a mistake.

He turned back around, his mask fully in place, but he refused to look at Sunny. It was too dangerous for him. "I'll have the lock removed. Meanwhile call Agnes. Tell her I said to set you up in whatever room you want at The Benton. I'll see you tomorrow for our dinner."

He started to go back to his car, but she surprised him by catching his arm.

"Let me go, Sunny," he said, keeping his voice monotone.

But she didn't let him go. "Something just happened. Something I said got to you, really got to you. Tell me what it was."

"Let me go, Sunny," he repeated.

"No, look at me, Cole."

He kept his head carefully turned away. "No."

"That's surprising," she answered, "I wouldn't have pegged you as the type of guy who couldn't look someone in the eye."

Of course he couldn't let her challenge go unanswered. It just wasn't in his nature. He turned back around, drew himself up and made himself look at her.

But dammit, her eyes...they were no longer blazing with fury. Now they were soft with pity. Like he was some kind of stray she'd found in the street. "I don't need your pity," he said.

She just shrugged. "Well, too bad. You've got it. Now do you want to talk about what's got you so shook up?"

"No," he said, his voice a final answer.

They stood there in silence while he waited for her to give up and let go of his arm, but instead she gripped it even tighter. Then she pressed her lips together and said the last thing he would have expected at that moment. "Okay, I have your terms."

Chapter 14

What just happened? Seriously, what just happened?
One minute Sunny had been two seconds away from
calling the police on Cole Benton, pretty damn sure she'd
unintentionally gotten tangled up with a stone-cold psycho. And the next, she was offering him the terms he'd
been demanding since Sunday.

Two minutes ago, she would have said, for sure, Cole
was the crazier person in this scenario, but now she didn't
know if it was him or her.

It had been the look on his face after she yelled having sex with him had been a mistake. He'd just looked
so... hurt. Truly hurt. Like she had kicked him somewhere down deep.

And now she just had to know what made a man
like Cole Benton look like that.

She was definitely the crazier one in this scenario,
and Cole was looking down at her as if he knew it, too.

"You're serious?" he said.

She nodded. "You want terms, and I've got them. Were you serious about honoring whatever I requested?"

"Mostly," he answered. "If you requested controlling ownership of my business, I'd have to negotiate you down to a few shares."

Sunny felt her eyes crinkle with amusement. "Why do I get the feeling that's your version of a joke?"

He didn't smile back, just stood there, staring down on at her. Like a hawk.

And she felt more than a little preylike. "My terms aren't negotiable, but they are reasonable."

He squinted in that Clint Eastwood way of his. "Define reasonable."

"You don't know me, and I don't know you, but I hope you believe me when I say I'm not a greedy person. I'd never ask you for anything you couldn't give, or anything I didn't think you were capable of giving."

"If I agree to honor these 'reasonable' terms of yours, you'll agree to not only share my bed, but also to never purposefully fall out of communication with me or disappear without telling me where you are?" His shrewd eyes roamed over her as if he were trying to scan her mind. Trying to figure her out.

Sunny was pinged by a pinprick of guilt. He honestly seemed upset by her ignoring him all day. Not just peeved, but unsettled. "Yes, I guess I can promise that," she answered.

Still he continued to scan her, his eyes going up and down over her face. "This isn't how I usually do business," he told her.

"Me, either, because once again, I'm not a hooker,

and I don't consider relationships to be business trans-actions. But obviously you do, so I'm putting this in 'terms' you can understand," she told him, not bothering to disguise how little she thought of the idea. "If it was up to me, I'd call it 'setting boundaries for our relationship going forward.'"

He frowned, and chose that moment to finally take his arm back. "Fine, I pre-agree to your terms."

"Seriously?" she said not hiding her surprise. "Without even hearing what they are?"

"Yes, seriously," he answered.

Sunny found herself having to take a deep breath, a really deep breath "Okay if you want me to sleep with you, I'm going to need three things." She held up her index finger. "One, you can't threaten my friends. It's not nice and I don't want to have to worry about them every time I do or say something you don't like. This side deal is between you and me and everybody else gets left out of it. No punishing them to get to me."

He folded his arms. "Fine," he huffed. "But if you don't do or say anything I don't like, then punishments won't be an issue."

She rolled her eyes. "If you want somebody who won't ever do or say anything you don't like, then you can just go ahead and get an escort, which let me remind you again, I'm not."

"I said, fine," he said, looking irritated. "What's your two of three?"

"Two," she said, uncurling her middle finger to join the index. "You can't be horrible to me anymore."

He shook his head. "I didn't think I was being horrible to you. In fact, it seemed like just the opposite last night in the hotel room."

She felt her cheeks warm. For having such an icy exterior, the man sure knew how to make a girl blush. But still she insisted. "You've got to at least try to be nice to me. That's all I'm asking, that you try your best to be nice."

"How do I know when I'm not being...*nice?*" He said the last word as if it put a bad taste in his mouth.

"I'll let you know," she assured him.

Was that a glint of amusement in Cole Benton's eyes? It flitted in and out so fast, she wasn't sure if she was just imagining it.

"Fine. I'll try to be nice. And you'll let me know if I'm in violation of your terms."

Somehow he made the phrase *violation of your terms* sound way sexier than it should have.

"What's your number three?" he asked, and this time she could clearly see a smile playing around on his lips.

But Sunny uncurled her ring finger, anyway. "Three!" she said. "You've got to talk to me. This clamming up when I ask you a question isn't going to cut it."

Cole's amused look disappeared. "I'm not a talker," he said.

"Well, I am," she answered. "And if you want to do this with me, you've got to get cool with talking to me. You know, communication?"

Maybe he didn't know, because he was looking at her as though she had just used a completely foreign word.

"Communicate? It's this thing that people who aren't in psycho relationships do?" she explained

"Yes, I had a therapist when I was a kid. I know

what communication is," he answered, his voice flat. "But it's not something I'm comfortable with. For example, what happened earlier. That's not something I can talk with you about. I don't talk about that."

All sorts of questions came to Sunny's mind, including why he had needed a therapist when he was younger? And why couldn't he talk about what just happened?

Though she did realize that she was asking a lot of him after only a few days of knowing each other. "That's cool. You don't have to talk about it, but do your best when I ask you about your stuff, okay?"

"Okay," he answered and he held out his hand to her. "I'll do my best, and we have a deal."

It was a statement, not a question, and it sent a ripple of fear through Sunny's heart, filling her with hesitation. Was she really going to do this? Was she really going to pretend to be Cole Benton's girlfriend, and also share his bed?

After a few moments of hesitation, she found herself shaking his hand. "We have a deal," she told him. Then she grimaced. "But we'll have to wait to make it official. I got waxed today."

Chapter 15

If Sunny thought negotiating a no-strings-attached summer fling with Cole Benton had been weird, it was nowhere near as awkward as what came next.

They drove back in separate cars, plenty of time for Sunny to go back and forth with herself, wondering what the hell she was doing and why she was doing it. Would Cole even keep up his side of the bargain? And what would she do if he didn't? The thoughts and what-ifs kept piling up in her head like a horrific car wreck, and by the time she got into Cole's private elevator, she was about ready to call the whole thing off. Tell him she'd changed her mind.

The elevator doors whispered open inside his penthouse, and there was Cole, tie now off, the top buttons of his shirt undone, hair askew, as though he'd run his hand through it several times while waiting for her to arrive.

He immediately pulled her to him and kissed her...
and...and what had Sunny been planning to do as soon
as she got to the penthouse? She melted into him, suddenly unable to remember.

"Don't change your mind," he commanded. Then
as if remembering their conversation from earlier he
added the most terse "Please" she'd ever heard.

"Okay," Sunny said, wondering if he had a mind
scrambler somewhere on his body, because she never
seemed to be able to think straight when she was in
his presence. Especially when he touched her.

"Tonight separate bedrooms. I don't think I can—"
He broke off, and a shadow fell over his face. "I've
already had enough self-control fails today. I'd rather
not add another one to the list."

Sunny wondered if she'd ever get used to how angry
Cole seemed to feel about the whole situation. Most
guys would love getting an NSA relationship, especially one with a woman who was guaranteed to leave
at the end of the summer, no harm, no foul. Also, he
had gotten nearly exactly what he'd asked for. But
the further he got with her, the angrier it seemed to
make him.

Still, it was nice to know she wasn't the only one
overwhelmed by this situation. Obviously she was
getting to him like he was getting to her.

"Okay," she agreed quietly. "I'll go back to the
room I stayed in before."

He took another step back from her, as if he had
to physically restrain himself from jumping on her
right there in the living room. Maybe he did? Sunny
thought to herself, feeling weirdly complimented by
the possibility.

"On weekdays I work from six to nine, then I go down to our main restaurant for breakfast. My way of assuring that the staff is at their best every day."

Sunny grinned. "Also, yum, breakfast."

"You should join me."

Sunny looked down at the capri yoga pants and tank top she wore. "This is all I have to wear right now. *Somebody* locked all my clothes up inside my apartment."

"I'll have Agnes send something up," Cole answered, sounding the slightest bit amused.

"Thank you," she said, sensing it would be useless to argue with him. Luckily this was Vegas where anything could be gotten at any time of the night, so at least she knew she wouldn't be putting poor Agnes out more than she already had.

She didn't expect to wake up to a living room filled with boxes and wardrobe bags all emblazoned with the names of stores she'd never step foot in because she knew she couldn't afford anything they were selling. The sight was enough to jolt her awake, no first-thing morning coffee needed.

And after a casual inventory of the items, she saw that it wasn't just stuff for her to wear when she was out and about with Cole. There were also exercise clothes, jeans, loungewear and underwear, lots and lots of underwear. Enough bra and panty sets to stock an entire Victoria's Secret fashion show, including silk teddies. Sunny's cheeks went into total burn mode

"The clothes are too much," she told Agnes when Cole's assistant called to get her breakfast order. Apparently Cole didn't like to waste even the time it took to put in an in-person order. "I won't be needing most of this stuff. Can I just pick out a couple of things to get me through until my apartment gets unlocked and send the rest back?"

"If Mr. Benton approves that request, I'll be happy to arrange that for you."

Sunny twisted her mouth, seeing exactly what Agnes did there. "But there's like no way he'd approve it, right?"

"It's not my place to speak for Mr. Benton, but no, I highly doubt it." She could tell Agnes was laughing at her on the other end of the call.

"Can I ask if this is usual? Like does he always buy entire wardrobes for the women he dates?"

She could sense Agnes's hesitation, and Sunny wondered if she'd even answer. But then Agnes lowered her voice and said, "The truth is, most of the women Mr. Benton dates come with designer wardrobes. The full package, so to speak. I've never had to arrange for a toothbrush for one of Mr. Benton's dates, much less a wardrobe."

"Oh, okay," Sunny answered feeling queasy in her stomach. "Well, thanks for mine, then. It's um…really nice." She quickly hung up the phone, wondering why Cole was so set on having her. Agnes had just confirmed once again that she definitely wasn't his usual type.

Breakfast with Cole was just like she suspected breakfast with Cole would be. He spent most of it either staring out the window as though he'd rather be somewhere else or checking his phone. He didn't say much, and all the while Agnes's words rang in her ears.

The truth is most of the women Mr. Benton dates come with designer wardrobes. The full package, so to speak.

Sunny stood up, her breakfast only half-finished.

"Where are you going?" he asked, looking at her directly for the first time since she'd arrived.

"I don't know," she answered, fingering the diagonal ruffle on the coral colored silk romper she'd decided to wear to breakfast. "I was thinking of going to the community center and working on the routine for Sunday's class. Or maybe I'll pay Nora a visit, pretend to actually do my job."

He gave her a sharp look, before checking his phone yet again. "We still have thirteen minutes left for breakfast."

Sunny shrugged. "Sorry, I guess getting ignored for most of the hour has killed my appetite."

A beat passed, and then Cole very deliberately set down his phone. "You think I'm ignoring you?" he asked her.

"I don't have to think anything. I've been living it for the last seventeen minutes," she answered.

"Sit down."

Sunny opened her mouth to argue, but he cut her off with a reminder. "We're in public, Sunny."

She sat down. He was right. Getting into a petty argument in public wouldn't exactly sell their romance.

When she was once again seated, she waited for him to lambaste her for almost making a scene, but instead he leaned forward. "You have great legs. Actually you have great everything, but the outfit you're wearing really highlights your legs."

"Thank you," she said carefully, appreciating the

unexpected compliment, but wondering where it was coming from.

"I want those legs around my waist, holding on to me tight while I take you. Seeing you in that outfit, it's all I can think about."

Momentarily Sunny was struck speechless. "And that's why you keep checking your phone? Because of my legs?"

He picked up his phone and turned it toward her. There was a clock open on it, one that was running backward. Sunny squinted at it in confusion, not understanding why he was showing her this particular screen. But then she realized that when the clock ran out it would be one o'clock. Twenty-four hours since she'd left the Benton Spa directly after getting waxed.

"You're ah…" She couldn't finish, she was so embarrassed.

"Highly anticipating taking a late lunch today," he answered. He put his phone back in his breast pocket. "You think I'm ignoring you. I'm doing everything in my power to keep my hands off of you."

Sunny couldn't hide the wicked smile that came to her face. She, too, was more than a little turned on by the prospect of hooking up with Cole again. She'd thought about it all night and most of the morning. So it was nice to know she wasn't the only one affected by the delay.

She slipped her foot out of her shoe. "I'm sorry to hear you're suffering, Cole." She raised her leg and pressed her foot lightly into Cole's crotch. "But here, maybe I can help you…"

She kept her body language casual for the outside world, but she pressed her foot even farther between

Cole's legs and was instantly rewarded when she felt him go hard underneath the bare pad of her foot.

"Sunny..." he said.

She pulled her foot away and put it back in her shoe with a saucy smile. "Sorry, I probably shouldn't have done that. Wouldn't want you to lose control."

His eyes were hot on hers now. "I'm going to let you leave our breakfast date early, then take a few minutes before I go back to my office. A nurse will be visiting you to draw blood within the hour. Go do whatever you want with your day after that, but no matter what you do..." He leaned forward. "Be back in the penthouse by one."

A chill went down Sunny's back, an incongruously hot one, and she felt herself clench down below in anticipation. She smiled, rising from the table. "Okay, see you later, Cole."

She then walked away from their breakfast table, now thinking that her not being his usual type might not be such a bad thing.

Chapter 16

Cole didn't get into his private elevator until five after one, simply to prove that he could wait. He needed to believe that he still had some control over this situation with Sunny, even if he'd been compulsively checking his countdown clock all day.

But delaying his arrival wasn't a good decision on his part.

Sunny wasn't in the living room, or in the guest bedroom. He was just about to call her phone, demanding to know where she was and when the hell she was coming back when he heard her whisper, "Cole, is that you?"

Her voice was coming from his room, and when he threw open the door he found her, sitting on top of his bed, with her knees tucked in front of her. Completely naked.

"I really liked that romper, too," she explained,

pointing toward where she'd carefully laid it out over the back of one of the room's black side chairs. "So I took it off. I didn't want you hurt it."

She was totally serious, he realized, when she followed this explanation up with a nervous nibble on her lip, peeking up at him as if she wasn't sure what his reaction would be to finding her naked in his bed.

But how could she not know? Bountiful breasts, wide hourglass hips, framing what he suspected was a very generous backside. He liked what he saw all right. Apparently, even after breakfast, she still wasn't quite grasping just how sexy she was to him.

He became hard as a battering ram inside his pants. It had been a bad, stupid, terrible decision to wait even five minutes longer than necessary to come up there.

He'd promised himself that he'd punish her long and hard for teasing him the way she had at breakfast. He'd even told Agnes not to disturb him for the next hour, so that nothing could interfere with his erotic revenge.

But seeing her without a stitch of clothing in his bed…her heavy breasts out, their nipples pebbled, left no doubt that no matter how difficult it had been to get her here, she definitely wanted to be there now. He found himself having to look away for a few seconds, closing his eyes while he tried to get control of himself.

Control, control, control, that's the most important thing, he reminded himself. This was all supposed to be about control. Taking back control of a situation that had gotten wildly out of hand. Conquering it before it could conquer him.

"Cole? Is everything all right?" He could hear her moving to sit up, a note of worry in her voice.

Cole was grateful for it. He hated the look of pity she had given him the night before, and even more so, the note of concern he now heard in her voice. It gave him the fuel to do what he wanted to do without his runaway lust getting in the way.

He opened his eyes and let her see just how cold they'd gone.

To Sunny it was like seeing Cole morph from a man into an ice sculpture. She'd delighted in Cole's reaction to her at first. The way his eyes had heated up, showing her that she wasn't the only one who'd spent the day in the grips of some pretty hardcore sexual anticipation.

But then that familiar anger had come back, flashing across his face before he turned away from her, closing his eyes. And when he opened them again, the cool and controlled businessman was back in full effect, even colder than he'd been on that first day when they'd met in his office.

Sunny scooted back on the bed feeling very self-conscious. Putting herself on naked display on top of Cole's bed had been a bad idea. She could see that now. Too much, too soon. No wonder he was giving her the icicle treatment now.

She reached for the blanket and tried to cover herself up, but Cole was across the room in an instant, his hand clamping around her wrist before she could even shield her breasts.

He held her there from his standing position at the edge of the bed, his green eyes running over her body like a scientist's. "Show me."

Sunny froze. "Show you what?"

"Spread your legs, Sunny. Show me the reason I was kept waiting."

Sunny swallowed. Another command, this one impossibly intimate. Expose herself even more. One Sunny didn't know if she could honor, not with the serious doubts now running through her head.

But somehow she made herself do it, uncurl her legs and spread them out for him. His gaze stayed on her the whole time, so strong it felt as if it was the power of his stare pushing her legs apart.

The only indication Cole gave that he was in any way affected by what he saw was the tightening of his hand around her wrist, right before he let it go.

He laid his hands down on the inside of her thighs, just below her V. Then…nothing.

He just stood there, looking at her, and she became deeply aware of her body's response to his stare. She could feel herself start to throb, the lips of her entrance pulsing in and out, as wetness pooled at her center, and that made her feel even more exposed, even more naked than before.

She attempted to close her legs, but he easily kept them spread apart. In fact, he pushed down and spread her legs even farther apart, brushing his thumb lightly against the lips of her cleft as he did so. And a piercing arrow of sexual need shot through Sunny's core.

"Was it worth it?" he asked her, his voice low and rough.

Sunny didn't even try to answer. Just watched him watch her.

"Do you like lying here completely exposed to me?"

Another hard question to answer. Technically the answer was no. Sunny had never felt this uncomfortable in her life. All she wanted was to get away from him and his unwavering stare, but on the other hand....

She could feel herself involuntarily clenching and unclenching now. Practically begging Cole.

He answered her body's silent plea, moving his hand to cover her now glistening mound.

Sunny moaned when his fingers found her slit, and she arched into the pads of them as he ran them up and down, tantalizing her, but not quite touching her in the way she needed to be touched. He didn't put his fingers inside her the way he had in the hotel room on Sunday.

Now her embarrassment gave way to frustration. "Why are you torturing me?" she asked. "I thought this was what you wanted."

"It is," he answered, matter of fact. "But I also want you to understand what will happen if you ever tease me again like you did at breakfast."

Understanding bloomed inside her mind. So he was punishing her for teasing him. Well, two could play that game. "Torturing me because I gave you blue balls falls under the 'not nice' clause," she informed him breathlessly. "You're in violation of our agreement."

An impressed smile played along his lips. "You want me to be nice to you, Sunny?"

He brought two of his fingers just to the outside of her tunnel, pressing against its entrance, but not pushing the two digits through. Sunny hissed, her belly caving in with need before she arched herself into him, desperately trying to get him inside her.

It worked. Sort of.

He pushed in, maybe about an inch and stopped short. "Is this nicer, Sunny?"

"More," she moaned.

He pushed in a little more. But not nearly far enough. Frustrated, Sunny let out a whimper of disappointment.

"Sunny, you seem upset," she heard him say above her.

"Because…you won't. You won't.…"

"Say it, Sunny. If you want me to be nice, tell me what you want."

"I want you to push them in. All the way in."

"Like this," he asked.

He suddenly rammed his fingers inside of her all the way to his second set of knuckles, and for a moment it felt glorious, as though she was getting exactly what she wanted. But once again, he didn't move.

"Move your fingers. Please, move them," she demanded.

He didn't move his fingers. Not even a wiggle. And when she tried to move her own hips, his other hand still on her thigh, pressed down, so that she couldn't.

She brought her own hand down to her core, bitterly disappointed, but more than used to having to take care of her own needs.

He knocked it away. Then he just stood there, so long her body started to scream with sexual frustration.

"Not nice," she moaned, her hands coming up to her own breasts, now heavy and swollen with need. She palmed them, tugging on her own nipples. She felt as if she was losing it, and closed her eyes, so that she didn't have to see him watching her with that slight smirk on his face as she came completely undone.

"So not nice," she panted. "You're watching me humiliate myself. And it's so not nice—"

He suddenly started pistoning his fingers inside of her and then his mouth came crashing down on her core, wet and hot.

Her back arched. The combination of his mouth and his fingers felt like the most erotic sex dream come true.

"Oh, Cole," she whimpered. "That feels so good. So good!"

She didn't last long under his double assault. She came in a blaze of heat, all the way from the top of her pelvis to the bottom of her toes.

And then he was on top of her, once again kissing her as he hauled her up higher in the bed. He unzipped his pants and Sunny cried out with pleasure. He filled her up completely, sinking in deep. It felt so nice to have him like this. Sunny guessed that he must have gotten word that her blood test came back clear before he'd arrived at the penthouse.

He obviously liked the feel of being unsheathed inside of her, too. He drilled into her, with a thrust that could easily be described as punishing. But it no longer felt anything like a punishment to Sunny, and she held onto him tight, more than happy to receive him.

"Get them around me," he said, his voice now ragged and hoarse. "Your legs…get them around me, and come, Sunny, come."

She did as he instructed, and this new position exposed her clit to his thrusts in a way it hadn't before. She came almost immediately, her yellow nails digging into his suit jacket. Then he came soon after with an angry lion roar, his cock jerking inside of her.

After he was done, he rose up, looking down at her, his light green eyes filled with tenderness, and for a moment they melted Sunny's heart.

But in the next moment, his eyes frosted over, and Ice Sculpture Cole came back. He moved away from her. "I should get back to work," he said.

He started to redo his pants, and then stopped and said, "Actually, I should take a shower first."

He took his phone out and set it on the nightstand before he began stripping out of his suit.

A chill ran all the way through Sunny, pinning her heart to the back of her chest. What he meant was that he needed to get her smell off of him. Erase all traces of what they'd done before he went back to work. And what had been so beautiful for Sunny just a few moments before became ugly. So ugly, tears formed in her eyes, without warning.

She forced them back down, turning her head away, so that Cole wouldn't see how much he'd hurt her. *Hold on, just hold on for a few seconds,* she told herself. The coast would be clear after he disappeared into the bathroom. Then she'd be free to run out and cry like a not very big girl in her room without him ever being the wiser. She waited for the click of the bathroom door.

But the click never happened, and eventually she heard his footsteps as he came back across the room to stand at the right side of the bed. She could feel him standing there, watching as she tried not to cry.

"I thought you were going to take a shower," she said, when too many excruciating seconds had passed.

She raised her head to take a quick look at him, and found him standing there in nothing but a bath towel, as if he'd thought about going ahead and taking his shower, but had decided to come back out there and talk to her instead.

"What's wrong?" he asked, sounding more than a little aggrieved.

"Nothing," she answered.

"Sunny, remember what I told you about how I felt about you lying to me?"

She did remember that. She took a deep breath and confessed, "I have some issues, I guess. Big ones that I should have thought about before agreeing to this arrangement."

Issues. Good one. If there was ever a way to send a man as all business as Cole running for the hills, it was to freely admit that she had major issues.

But the next thing she felt was the bed depressing under his weight. "I'm not good at this," she heard him say beside her. "But I agreed, so yeah, okay. Let's do this. Let's *talk*."

He said this in the same way a child would say, "Okay, sure, put a big heap of vegetables on my plate." And that only mad Sunny feel worse.

"No, you don't have to talk to me. I'm not asking you to talk to me right now. You—you don't have to do that. Just go to work. I'll be fine…"

No movement at all came from his side of the bed. "Are you upset because I punished you for teasing me?"

"No, that was…actually that was kind of hot."

"Then why are you crying?"

"I'm not crying," she insisted.

But Cole saw right through her. "Fine. Then why are you trying not to cry?"

"Seriously, Cole. I don't want to have this conversation with you. Just go. When you get home from work, I'll be fine. I promise."

She couldn't do this anymore. She had to get out of there. Blinking the unshed tears out of her eyes, she made a move to get up, only to have Cole catch her wrist for the second time that afternoon.

"So the deal is I have to talk to you, but you don't have to talk to me?" he asked.

Now she turned to confront him. "You still haven't told me why you got upset last night," she reminded him, yanking on her wrist.

"So it's an exchange. I tell you what you want to know and you tell me what's going on with you?"

"No! That's not what I'm trying to say—" she broke off with an exasperated huff. "Not everything's a perfect business exchange, Cole. You're asking me to talk to you, and I'm telling you it's not worth talking about. Please let go of me."

His hand stayed circled around her wrist. "I'll be the judge of that."

"No, you won't, because I don't want to talk about it," she said, feeling slightly hysterical. "Okay? I don't."

He stared at her for a few cold seconds, and then he said, "My mother said I was a mistake. That having me was a *mistake*. She was drunk and angry years later, because my father had left her for another woman— Max's mother. She told me I ruined her body, made my father stop looking at her like a woman. Maybe she had a point, because he eventually left Max's mother, too. But my mother died right after she said that to me—took a spill into our pool and drowned—so there you go."

Sunny covered her mouth with her hand, her eyes wide.

"And there's the look of pity again," he said, dropping her wrist. "That's why I didn't want to tell you last night."

"I'm not a block of stone, Cole. No mother should ever say that to her child and I'm sorry, truly sorry, that was said to you."

Cole made a hurry up motion with his hand, winding it around in a circle. "Can we talk about your thing now?"

Sunny pursed her lips. It was true that this wasn't supposed to be yet another business exchange, but Cole has just shared something painful with her, something he obviously hadn't told a lot of people, if anyone. And it felt peevish not to just push down her self-consciousness and fess up.

She crossed her arms across her chest. "When you went cold on me right after we finished and decided to take a shower, it reminded me of my ex," she mumbled.

Cole's face went blank in a way she could tell was very deliberate. "Your ex, the do-gooder."

"Yeah, him."

"I reminded you of the guy who wastes his time trying to shame people into volunteering their time outside of grocery stores as opposed to paying employees what they're worth to come work at the shelter he runs."

"Well, no, you don't remind me of him when you

talk like that, like the least altruistic man on earth. But when you can't wait to get into a shower after you have sex with me, then yeah, you do."

Cole, who Sunny was beginning to think was incapable of feeling insult unless the word *mistake* was used, just raised his eyebrow. "Why?"

"He didn't want to be seen with me. He said dating a showgirl wasn't a good idea for a man in his position. He claimed to love me, but he kept me hidden, like a dirty secret. And he, um, always used to shower right after. Like he needed to clean me off of him."

"So when did you figure out he was married?"

Sunny's eyes went wide again. "Pru saw him with his wife, walking their dog, after one of her brother's soccer games. How did you know he was married?"

"That's the only real reason any man wouldn't want to be seen with you," Cole answered.

And Sunny found herself in the weird position of having to hold back her laughter after her tortured confession. "Really. The only reason? I mean, I'm black, too. How about racism? I'm not everybody's cup of tea."

"The only reason," Cole repeated, like it was a matter of fact and not simply his opinion. Then he frowned. "So now what do we do? Talk about why I was going to take a shower and go back to my office. Is that how it works?"

Sunny scrunched up her face, not knowing if she'd ever get used to the way Cole saw everything as a business discussion. "Yeah, I guess that's kind of how it works."

Cole turned his eyes to the tinted window with its view overlooking the east side of the Strip. "I'm pissed off at myself right now. I planned to tease you for a while—I didn't even make it to the end of my lunch hour."

Sunny laughed, but then she realized…he was totally serious. "You went cold on me, because you couldn't torture me for as long as you were planning?"

"I don't think you took me seriously when I told you I like to be in control," he said, his jaw setting.

"No, I didn't," she said. "Because who cares what you want?" Before he could stop her, she used her dancer's muscles to quickly push herself up and over his body, straddling him and settling into his lap in one smooth move. "If that was Cole Benton out of control, that's who I want to be sharing a bed with from now on."

"How do you know?" he asked. "So far I haven't been able to stay in control where you're concerned."

As if to prove his point, she felt him swell underneath his towel.

"Mmm," she said with a delighted chuckle. "Tell me more."

He shook his head, as if this conversation was exasperating him, as if she was totally exasperating him. "Sunny, I didn't even get my suit jacket off, I didn't get my shoes off."

She gave him another look of pity, one he couldn't possibly take offense to because it was nowhere near real. "Poor baby. Well, at least you don't have to worry about that this time, because there's nothing between us but this towel."

She let her chest fall against his, and her nipples pebbled as she rubbed them against his rock-hard pecs.

She couldn't help but appreciate the fact that he was hard, everywhere she was soft.

In some cases really hard. His erection rose up through the towel's crease, poking against her slit in a way that made her instinctively adjust herself, so that all he had to do was push in.

Which he did.

Sunny moaned. He was even thicker inside her in this position, filling her up in a way that felt both pleasurable and impossible, because how in the world could something that big feel so good inside her.

"Sunny…" he said, his hands circling her waist.

"So you wouldn't mind if I started doing this?" She rocked her hips, gliding up and down on his thick erection, taking what she wanted as brazenly as she wanted to.

Cole rewarded her with a sharp intake of breath, his head falling back against the headboard.

Sunny leaned forward, taking him in even farther as she giggled in his ear. "Oh, no, I seem to be teasing you again, keeping you here, when all you wanted to do was get back to the office and work some more."

She braced herself with her hands on his shoulders and worked her core, rising up and sitting down in a way that she hoped was as pleasurable for him as it was for her—at least pleasurable enough to bring back the out of control Cole.

The cold businessman was fine to talk to, and though she'd cursed him while he was teasing her, she had to admit that the orgasm he revved up in her with just his fingers had been earth-shattering. But when it came to doing the deed, to having Cole Benton's hard length inside of her, she didn't want the cold and civilized businessman, she wanted the beast inside of him.

She soon got exactly what she wanted. Just a few strokes in, he grabbed her around the waist and flipped her over onto her back, pounding into her with such force she knew he'd lost all control again. Knew it and thanked the stars for it. Cole was relentless on top of her, forcing himself in and out of her quivering core until he finally growled at her to come.

She did. Hard. So hard, it sent Cole over the edge, too.

He cursed and once again spilled into her, his body shaking as he emptied out.

But this time when he tried to pull out, Sunny brought her legs up and laced them around her waist.

"Oh, no, what did I do?" she asked with faux alarm. "You were supposed to be taking a shower, and I got you even dirtier. Now I've given you something else to be mad at me about."

Against all odds, she felt him harden again inside of her, and he shook his head. "What are you trying to do to me?"

She batted her eyelashes. "I guess I'm just a naughty girl, when it comes to you, Cole. A really, really naughty girl. You might have to punish me extra hard when you get home from work."

His face iced over and he reached for the phone he'd put on the nightstand when he'd taken his suit off.

"Um…what are you doing?" Sunny asked, feeling decidedly less vixenish as she watched him type out a message with one hand.

"Texting Agnes to clear my calendar for the day," he answered. Then he tossed the phone onto a nearby pillow. "I'm going to punish you extra hard, *right now.*"

And that he did.

Chapter 17

"You wore the new coral romper. On purpose?" he asked when Sunny sat across from him at the lunch table two weeks later.

Sunny flashed him a knowing smile as she opened her menu. The original romper had died an early death a few days beforehand when Sunny had made the mistake of bringing him dinner in his office, when he'd stayed late to clear out his inbox after sending Agnes home. Not only had the dinner gone uneaten, the emails ended up having to wait until the next morning, at which time he'd also asked Agnes to order a replacement romper stat.

Apparently the replacement had made it to Sunny, but she'd chosen not to wear it until their weekly lunch at The Benton's Golf Club.

He shook his head at her. "You're lucky we're in

public. I'll be seeing you and that romper by close of business."

"Actually, I have plans with Nora tonight. We're going to eat dinner here, and then go see the seven o'clock *Benton Girls* show."

"You're going to have to cancel," he said.

Sunny pursed her lips at him. "I'm supposed to be Nora's assistant, and we're lucky she brought your story about needing me to fake assist her, so that I could keep on getting paid and date you."

Not as lucky as Sunny believed. Nora had been too happy to go along with Cole's proposed plan, believing that he had fully caved in to her wishes to pursue Sunny as a wife. And it set Cole's teeth on edge knowing that she thought she'd gotten away with threatening him.

"She'll be fine without you," he said. "She's been going to *The Revue* without you all these years."

"That's what she said!" Sunny frowned. "But you're the one who said she needed the extra assistance, remember."

Cole's mood darkened. Yes, he did remember, and he cursed himself for adding in that extra detail now.

"Plus, who knows how much longer she'll even have to go to shows? The least I could do is go with her. Make sure she doesn't overdo it. Though, that's hard. Every time I try to help her during my visits, she keeps telling me she can do everything herself." Sunny's eyes went soft with fondness for his grandmother. "She's so brave."

Cole had to resist the urge to roll his eyes. "Like I said, she has her good and bad days."

Sunny's face suddenly lit up. "How about you come with us?"

Cole shook his head. "That's not in the original outing agenda, and I'd rather front-load my work, since I'm going with you to your dance class on Sunday." Which wouldn't be so bad, if he thought he'd be able to keep himself from giving in to the temptation to strip off Sunny's pink leotard ensemble as soon at they got back to the penthouse. Last Sunday, they'd ended up spending most of the morning in bed, and he hadn't made it into the office until well after lunch.

"Please?" Sunny said, fingering the ruffle on her romper and peeping up at him. "It would make Nora so happy to see you, and besides you owe me one."

He lifted his eyebrow. "Why do I owe you one?"

She lifted her eyebrow right back. "Pru and me went for our Monday Mani yesterday, and when I asked about getting waxed, I was informed that I didn't have access to any of their waxing services."

"Not when I'm in town," he said coolly.

"Yeah, they said that, too. Pru thought it was funny." Her eyebrow went even higher. "I didn't."

Cole felt no remorse about what he'd done to ensure he'd never have to go through that twenty-four hour wait time again. But he ran the calculation and decided to give in if it meant calling things even with Sunny. These past two weeks had been better than he'd expected. Way better.

Sunny wasn't just sexy, she was interesting. Pleasant and challenging at the same time, in ways that not only kept Cole coming back for more, but made it hard for him to spend as much time at the office as he used to, when he knew she was waiting for him in the penthouse.

He found himself not wanting to disturb the equilibrium they'd established over the past few weeks.

So that was how Cole ended up having dinner with Nora and the woman he was now pretending was his girlfriend in order to keep his grandmother from giving her shares to his brother.

But his resignation to eating dinner with the relative he could barely stand to look at these days turned into feeling as though luck was truly on his side when Nora came shuffling into the restaurant, slightly stooped over.

"Sorry, I'm late, luvs," she called out as she approached them. "Max showed up just as I was leaving. He's a terrible one for arriving to your doorstep without any notice, that one."

"Nora!" Sunny said, her eyes filled with worry. Both she and Cole stood up. Cole because Nora expected gentlemanly behavior when she joined him at a table, and Sunny in a rush to take Nora by the arm and help her into the booth. "You could have postponed if you were—" she exchanged a look with Cole "—having a bad day."

"I'm fine, I'm fine," Nora insisted. "Just a little tight around the edges. Besides I've never a missed a second Tuesday of the month with my Benton Girls yet, and I'm not going to let Dr. Aguila get in the way of my fun—or my Old Fashioneds," she added behind her hand.

And right on cue, a waiter showed up and set one of the bourbon cocktails his grandmother favored down in front of her with a smile and a warm greeting for Nora.

Cole knew "tight around the edges" meant Nora was recovering from yet another cosmetic procedure, and that Dr. Aguila was her long time plastic surgeon, but Sunny didn't have to know that.

"I think Dr. Aguila is right, *Gran*," he said, nodding toward the Old Fashioned. "You should probably lay off the booze tonight. No accounting for how it might react with your other medications."

Nora beamed. "He called me Gran?" she said to Sunny. "He never calls me Gran." She reached over and squeezed Sunny's cheek. "See, I knew you would be a good influence on him!"

Sunny could barely keep the distressed look off her face. And Cole could barely keep the sly smile off of his.

Chapter 18

"What?" Sunny asked with befuddled confusion, when the valet told her he couldn't bring the Mercedes around.

"Sorry, miss," the valet answered. "But I've already put in a call to Tomas. He'll be here with a car in just a moment."

"What the hell, Cole?" she said less than five minutes later when she was ensconced in the back of his Bentley, like some kind of helpless idiot who couldn't get herself from Point A to Point B. "Why'd you take away my car privileges?"

"I warned you about teasing me out in public," Cole answered, not even trying to hide his amusement on the other side of the line.

"Oh, my gosh, I don't wear panties to one little event…"

"And you choose not to inform me of that fact until we're in the middle of the *Benton Girls* show, with my grandmother sitting on the other side of me. You could have told me before we went downstairs to dinner."

"It wouldn't have been any fun if I told you then!" Sunny protested. "You're just mad because you've never done it in a bathroom before."

"I've also never had anyone whisper in my ear how wet she was for me. How she hoped her dress wasn't too short, because she didn't want to get her seat dirty—" He broke off with a curse. "Now I'm hard again. Tell Tomas to turn you around and bring you back here."

"No!" Sunny answered, her voice peevish. "Last night I promised your grandma I'd visit her today, and that's part of the plan, right? To go over there and go on and on about happy I am with you?"

A little shadow fell over Sunny's heart. Unfortunately that wouldn't be too hard of an act to pull off these days. As it turned out, the thing that had been missing from her life all these years was tons and tons of grade A sex with a hot businessman. As cold as Cole had come off when they first met, they'd been burning up his bedroom over the past couple of weeks, and the couch in the living room, and occasionally his office after Agnes had left for the day. And as of last night, the handicap stall in the women's bathroom at The Nora Benton Theater.

"She already knows you're into me. While you were lagging behind in the women's room, pretending we hadn't just had a quickie, I got to hear about how Nora and my grandfather used to the do the same thing when they first met. I had to hear a story about *my grandmother's sex life,* I'm pretty sure that means you owe *me* now."

"I do not owe you, Cole!" she said. "What am I going to do with you?"

"Tell Tomas to turn the car around and I'll give you explicit instructions about what you can do with me."

Now Sunny was turned on, and she actually thought about going back to The Benton.

However, she had promised Nora she'd visit, and she didn't want to be the kind of person who promised to visit a woman putting up a brave front as she faced down the last few months of her life, in order to have sex with—Sunny didn't know exactly what Cole was to her.

They were cohabiting, but they were only pretending to play the part of boyfriend-girlfriend in public, a fact that Sunny was keenly aware of, even if her heart insisted on beating a little faster whenever she caught him watching her from across the room.

It was only an act. She knew it was only an act, but…it just didn't feel like an act anymore. And that was how Sunny knew she was getting into dangerous territory where Cole Benton was concerned.

"I think you can wait until after my visit with Nora," she answered, putting more breeze in her voice than she actually felt. "I'll see you when you get off work."

"Lunch," he answered testily. "You'll see me at lunch. I'll have the restaurant send up our usual to the penthouse."

Their usual was sandwiches that could be eaten cold and quickly if Cole spent the majority of his lunch hour "punishing" her.

"Fine, we'll have a late lunch," she said. "See you then."

* * *

Nora lived in a gated community near the mountains in a stone manor that put Sunny in mind of English teas and horseback riding, even if Las Vegas was technically a desert—and even though the stables were only decorations.

"Never been one for horses. The truth is I can't stand the things," Nora had complained on Sunny's last visit after she'd given in to Sunny's suggestion to walk the grounds.

Cole hadn't talked much about what sort of illness Nora was battling, but Sunny knew from when her grandmother was passing on, that walks were universally prescribed until they couldn't be anymore. However, Nora had obviously been in pain the night before, wincing every time she had to get up or down. Who knew if she'd be having a good day or a bad day when she arrived.

Sunny hoped for the former as she knocked on the arched door at the front of the house. But when Nora's housekeeper answered the door, she gave Sunny an apologetic look. "Oh, I'm sorry, Miss Sunny, Mrs. Nora isn't here. Coovey fell down some stairs and she took him to the vet to get him checked out."

"Oh, no!" Sunny said. "I hope he's all right."

"Coovey's going to be fine," a voice said. Max appeared behind Nora's squat housekeeper, dressed in a T-shirt and jeans. "I'll take it from here, Suela."

Consuela moved out of the way with a parting nod and smile for Sunny, and Max stepped forward.

"Actually it's probably my fault you showed up here when you didn't have to," he told Sunny. "I think I might have said something like, 'Don't worry, Grandma, I'll call Sunny and cancel for you,' then I got distracted, and it must have slipped my mind."

"Oh," Sunny said, thinking it sounded as if it was definitely Max's fault she'd made the unnecessary trip. "Well, that's okay. I'll just head on home. Please tell Nora I'm thinking about her and Coovey. I hope he's all right."

Max waved it off. "Don't worry about it. That yapper is too mean to die. He'll probably outlive us all."

Sunny quickly covered her mouth with her hand to hide her smile. She'd never wish ill on any animal, but it was true, Nora's Jack Russell was more than a little yappy. She'd learned the first time she visited Nora a couple of weeks ago, that dressing defensively was the best way to avoid getting nipped by the small dog. One of the reasons Sunny had decided to wear thick socks and jeans, despite the infamous Las Vegas summer heat.

"Still, I know how much she loves Coovey," Sunny said, trying not to laugh. "Even if he is a yapper."

Max eyed her with approval. "So you're not a stick in the mud like every other girl Cole's dated. That's surprising…and disappointing."

Sunny shook her head, confused. "So you prefer stick in the muds?"

"Nope," Max answered. "But stick in the muds love me, especially the ones that go out with Cole. Guess I'm a refreshing change of pace, since I'm not…oh, I don't know, boring as hell."

He lifted his eyebrows, waiting for her to respond, and Sunny got a sense of what he must have been like as a kid, a flirtatious rascal in all things.

"Okay," she said carefully, keeping as far away from his bait as possible. "Well, like I said. No big deal. I'll see Nora next week."

"So according to Suela, you've been visiting my grandmother a lot lately, sometimes twice a week," he said, before she could turn to leave. "Is that part of your deal with Cole?"

"No," she answered.

He narrowed his eyes at her, and it reminded her of Cole, even though their personalities were on opposite ends of a spectrum. "Are you trying to get in good with my grandmother. Play her and my brother?"

Sunny blinked, suddenly realizing that he hadn't really just slipped and forgotten to call her. He had purposefully let her drive all the way out here, so that he could accuse her of being a gold digger on his grandmother's front porch.

"Okay," she said, holding up her hands. "I'm not even going to get offended, because that's your family and if I had any family left, I'd be protective of them, too. I'm just going to say that I'm not trying to play anyone. I love your grandmother, and I just want to spend as much time as possible with her before I leave. I'm not after anybody's money."

"Leave," Max repeated. "Where you going, Sunny?"

Sunny peeped over his shoulder to make sure Consuela wasn't anywhere around. Then she said, "Don't tell Nora, but I'm moving to New York at the end of summer. I've got a scholarship to study dance pedagogy in the fall."

Max stepped out of the house. "No idea what

dance pedagogy is, but you can tell me all about it over lunch."

He closed the door behind him and walked past her to the bright yellow Ferrari Tomas had parked behind in the manor's large, circular, white stone gravel drive.

"So Cole loaned you his Benny?" Max asked, nodding toward Tomas.

"No, long story, but it's kind of a joke," she answered. "And I already have lunch plans. I was only planning on visiting Nora for a little bit."

"Cancel them," he responded. He was reminding her more and more of Cole by the minute. He hitched his thumb at the Bentley. "So this the first time Tomas has ever driven you someplace alone?"

"Yes," Sunny answered.

"And Cole happened to play this 'joke' on you the day after I got into town," Max said.

She thought of all the things Cole had said about his brother in the back of the limo after their first official event, and she realized this might not have been as straightforward of a punishment as she thought when she first got in the Bentley.

"I'll definitely ask him about that when we meet for lunch," Sunny said.

"Or…" Max suggested, his wicked playboy eyes set to full gleam. "You could come to lunch with me in my car. It's a lot more fun than that old man Bentley.

"I'm not going anywhere with you," she told him.

Max waggled his eyebrows. "You sure about that? I got all the dirt on Cole, and I'm the only one who does. Or at least the only one who's not too scared of him to spill it."

Sunny hesitated.

Sorry can't make lunch, will make it up to you tonight.

Cole frowned when the message popped up across his screen. What did Sunny mean she couldn't make lunch? He'd known she'd been putting in more time at the community center, teaching more classes and coordinating the end-of-summer show for the girls. She'd even been trying to get him to take part in the show, since he'd been regularly coming with her to the Sunday classes. But she hadn't told him she was going anywhere today but to see Nora. And she'd never cancelled on him before.

On a hunch, he asked Agnes to get Tomas on the line.

"Hello, Mr. Benton. How can I help you?" Tomas said when Agnes put him through.

"Just a quick check in. Sunny just texted me that she couldn't make it back for lunch."

"*Sí*, she's still in the restaurant. I'm waiting outside."

Cole began to feel stupid for calling. Another non-controlled action Sunny had brought out in him. "I see, so she decided to go out to eat with Nora instead?"

"Ah…no, not exactly, Mr. Benton. I think something might have happened. Ms. Johnson said the plan was to go to lunch with your brother and she asked me to follow them to the restaurant. They've been in there for a little while. Do you want me to go get her? Give her a message? Mr. Benton? Mr. Benton?"

Cole didn't answer. Couldn't answer for a good number of seconds as his hand squeezed around the phone, tight as a chokehold. But finally he managed to squeeze out, "What restaurant?"

Tomas gave him the name of a little place, about five minutes from Nora's mansion, and Cole hung up without another word.

He then pushed the intercom button. "Agnes, have the valet bring one of my cars around."

Agnes must have heard the barely controlled rage in his voice, because she didn't ask which one like she usually did, just answered, "Right away, Mr. Benton."

Sunny didn't want to use the word *boring* to describe Cole's brother, but if the description fit.

His dirt turned out to be a total bust. Mostly stories that started off with Cole warning him not to do something and Max going on ahead and doing it, anyway, usually with disastrous results. He'd been telling her these stories for nearly an hour, and judging from the way he laughed at the end of all them, Max thought they were great. Somehow it was just hilarious to end up in jail in a foreign country or having to climb out of some married countess's window naked. The list went on and on, and convinced Sunny that Max wasn't exactly the international playboy as he'd been painted in the press. More like a rich guy with a knee-jerk need to rebel.

"So you don't work, like at all?" Sunny asked. "But the company is paying you to, what? Party all over the world?"

Max frowned as if he suspected she was purposefully trying to rain on his parade, but he pulled out his card, nonetheless, and handed it to her. "The official title is Brand Ambassador. I live the glamorous life all over the world and that reflects well on the hotel."

She inwardly grimaced. That wasn't what Cole had insinuated. But obviously Max had a much higher opinion of what he did for the company than Cole did.

"It sounds like you're putting your degree in marketing to use about as well as I did with my degree in dance over the last five years."

Max's forehead scrunched. "Why do I have the feeling that means 'not too well.' What's the matter, being a showgirl like our grandmas wasn't good enough for you?"

"Being a showgirl is great if you have the passion for it, and a lot of the women in *The Benton Girls Revue* do. But the truth is I took the easy way out. My boss was a friend of my grandma's and offered me a job as soon as I graduated. I took it, because I was too scared to pursue my dreams someplace where dancers didn't learn all their choreography in high heels." She took another sip of her iced tea. "It sounds to me like you're kind of scared, too, Max. Like you're running all over the world, acting like a jerk, so that you don't actually have to take any real chances."

The laughter disappeared from Max's eyes and he went still, so still, Sunny could once again see some of his brother in him. "You sound like my brother," he finally said.

Sunny had been on the wrong side of Cole's deadeyed stare enough times by now not to be intimidated by Max's version. She shrugged, "Okay, if making your brother the enemy helps you feel better about wasting your life, go with that. Whatever helps you get by."

"So you think I should be like Cole. Work all the time, never have any fun."

"I think you and Cole are on two opposite ends of the scale. He uses work to run away from his demons and you use fun."

Max glared at her. "What do you know about our demons?"

"Not a whole lot," Sunny admitted. "But they've got to be some kind of powerful to have you and Cole so shook."

Max shook his head. "You've said that? You've actually said that to my brother, and he's still with you?"

Sunny laughed, "No, not exactly. But I hope our relationship is helping him with his stuff. You know, like he's helping me with mine."

"You have *stuff*? I find that hard to believe."

"Why? Everyone has something going on, some of us are just better at hiding it. But you know, I was raised by Grandma, too, just like Cole."

"Yes, poor Cole who lost his mommy when he was a kid while I got to keep mine." Max cut his eyes away from her, staring off into space with a bitter expression. "What he doesn't get is that sometimes it's better if they die."

Recognizing a familiar bitterness in Max's words, Sunny reached across the table and took his hand. "I get that," she said softly. "I was raised by my grandmother, but my mom's still out there, walking the streets of God knows where, going after her next fix.

She's lost, and sometimes I think that might be even worse than her being dead, because she didn't want me—at least not as much as she wanted to get high."

Max's eyes met hers. "I'm sorry," he said. "Sorry about your mom, but just think, if she stayed like mine did, then you might have ended up like me. What did you call me? A waste?"

"No," Sunny said, rubbing the back of his hand. "You're not a waste. You're just a little lost. And you keep on touching base here in Las Vegas, so that's got to mean something."

"Yeah," Max said with a wry laugh. "That Cole insists I come home at least once a month to collect my paycheck. What a pain in the ass."

"Or…" Sunny said, tilting her head to the side, "you could look at it as an opportunity to reconnect with your brother. One chance every month. He's giving you that."

Max's eyebrows lifted and the wicked gleam returned to his eyes. "So you want me to what? Thank Cole for forcing me to come back to Las Vegas every month?"

Sunny was about to tell him it would be a start, when Max turned to look at something happening toward their left. His forehead scrunched up. "Is that Cole?"

Sunny looked up, too, just in time to see Cole, leaping like a Duke of Hazzard over the patio's low wrought-iron fence.

Everything happened fast after that. Cole got to their table in an instant, and the next thing Sunny knew, he was yanking Max out of his chair by the front of his T-shirt.

"No, Cole, don't!" she screamed.

But it was too late before Sunny could stop him, Cole hauled back and punched the hell out of his brother.

Chapter 19

Cole hadn't punched Max in years. Too long, really, and he got a certain amount of satisfaction when his fist came back with blood from his brother's split lip on it.

Blood Max spit out, like Cole's hit was nothing. He always had been able to take a punch like a pro fighter.

"Nice!" Max said, thumbing his jagged nose and raising his own fists with a wild blood-stained grin. "I was wondering when the *real* Cole would show up. Sunny, sweetheart, let me introduce you to him. I don't think you've met yet."

The only thing that kept Cole from punching Max right in the middle of his smug face again, was Sunny getting in his way before he could.

"Be careful, Sunny," Max warned. "You don't want him to lose it and hit you, too."

Cole tried to get around Sunny, ready to beat Max for as long as it took to make him stop talking, but Sunny put her hands on his chest.

"What did you say to me about causing scenes?" she asked, her eyes blazing with anger.

The world suddenly came back into focus for Cole then, and he looked up to see what Sunny was referring to. Lunch patrons—a whole lot of them, some with camera phones out, ready to record whatever he did next.

"Please, Cole, calm down," Sunny said, keeping her voice low. "Come back to the car with me and we'll talk."

After a few tense seconds, Cole grabbed her by the hand, dragged her through the main part of the restaurant and out the front door—there wasn't actually a patio entrance, which was why he'd been forced to jump the fence. But Cole didn't take her back to the car waiting for her in front of the restaurant, he took her to his Jag, which was still idling near the patio, the driver's-side door hanging wide-open, because he'd jumped right out of the car when he saw Max with Sunny, holding hands. Holding hands!

He opened the driver's-side door with a hard yank. "Get in," he told Sunny.

"You sure you want to go with him, Sunny Delight?" Max asked. He'd followed them out of the restaurant. "Hunting us down and punching me just for hanging out with you. That's a stalker move for sure. He's my brother, but you're one hell of a girl, and I'm not so certain you should be going home with him."

Max stood only a few feet away from them now, just outside of punching distance, but Cole could remedy that. He started toward him again, only to have

Sunny push him back. "No, Cole, don't make it worse than it already is." Then she looked over her shoulder at Max. "I'll be fine. Please just go, Max."

Max gauged the situation, looking from Sunny to Cole with a smirk. "Yeah, fine, I'll go. But, Sunny, if you need anything—" he pressed his palm to his chest and gave her a little bow in mock simulation of a true gentleman "—you know where to find me. I've just decided I'll be sticking around to help dear, sick Nora." His eyes clashed with Cole's. "At least until the end of the summer, then maybe I'll see you in New York."

Cole probably would have toppled Sunny over in his bid to get to Max if she hadn't dug her heels into the ground and used all her weight to keep him from moving forward. "Cole, no, I'll go with you, okay? Please just ignore him," she begged. "Please just get in the car or you'll ruin everything. If Nora hears about this…"

She was right. He had to get himself under control.

He breathed and breathed and breathed some more, until the red faded from his vision and he was left with nothing but ice-cold rage. A welcomed numbness that filled him up from head to toe.

He pointed to Max. "I'll deal with you later," he said in a way that let Max know it wasn't an empty threat.

He then said, "Get in the car," to Sunny as he went around to the driver's side with stone hard certainty that she would do exactly what he said.

They drove back to The Benton in complete silence, Cole staring dead ahead as if she weren't even in the car with him.

By the time they got to his private elevator, Sunny began to have several doubts about the wisdom of getting into another enclosed space with him.

She'd never seen him like this. It was worse than his usual ice-sculpture routine. In fact, it was like Ice Sculpture Cole on steroids, like Frozen Nitrogen Cole. Something so cold, Sunny was afraid it would burn to even touch him.

She thought maybe he'd go back to the office and leave her to return to the penthouse alone. But Cole pushed the P as the door slid closed.

"I know what it looked like. It looked like we were holding hands. But it wasn't like that," she told him. "We were talking, just talking."

Cole didn't say anything, which was somehow worse than him yelling or punching Max. It felt as if she was in the quiet eye of an incoming storm. Make that an incoming blizzard.

Sunny tried again. "You know, you and Max aren't that different. You just deal with what happened to you in different ways. And if you looked past your differences, I mean, really tried to talk to each other, you might find some common ground."

The elevator dinged and Cole held the door open so that she could disembark first. An unexpected gentlemanly gesture, and for a moment, Sunny thought she might have misread his mood. For a whole second. Then he grabbed her from behind, and the next thing Sunny knew her front was pressed into a nearby wall with Cole against her, the heavy length of his erection, hard against her back.

"The only common ground Max and I have is you, Sunny," he said into her ear. One hand disappeared up her shirt, finding her breast. Sunny gasped when his other hand found the front of her, cupping her core like it was his possession. "He wants to take you from me, and you gave him the perfect opportunity to do it...after promising me you wouldn't go anywhere near him."

Sunny shook her head in protest, not understanding why her body was responding to this, readying itself to receive him, even as she squirmed underneath his body and harsh words. "I didn't promise I wouldn't go near him. I said you didn't have to worry, and you don't because it was just lunch. I don't..."

Her breath hitched when he suddenly pulled back, leaving her there against the wall alone.

And when Sunny turned around it was to the sight of Cole, his face set in stone. But there was something ragged in his eyes now, a wildness that hadn't been there before.

"Cole?" She tentatively reached out for him.

But he took a step back from her, his body as stiff as a statue. Control, she realized. He was fighting for control. So hard, he wouldn't even let her touch him.

"Cole," she said again, her heart spiking with concern. But not for herself. For him.

That scene with Max had shaken him. Shaken him like that night they'd had the confrontation about her.

"Cole, what's this about?" she asked him.

"You promised," he answered. "You promised me you wouldn't go anywhere near him."

She shook her head at him. "Okay, say I promised—which I didn't. But say I did? What you did was out of line. Dragging me out of that restaurant, punching Max—"

"Max?" he said, his voice tight. "You're mad at me for punching Max? Max is exactly like his mother. He's lucky I didn't do worse."

"He's exactly like his mother," Sunny repeated, shaking her head. "What does that even mean? And what does that have to do with me?"

He turned his head away from her, his fist clenching and unclenching like he was dreaming about going after Max again. And when his eyes swung back around, the ragged look was gone, replaced by a look that was all business.

"Here's how this is going to go. I'm going to go downstairs and put in a call to my lawyer. He's going to draw up an addendum to our contract, one guaranteeing you won't talk to Max or be seen with him."

His mouth broke into a menacing snarl but his voice remained an icy monotone as he said, "And then I'm going to come back up here, and I'm going to have you, Sunny. Again and again until I forget about you having lunch with him. Until I can't see you holding his hand like you were a couple. Until you remember exactly whose bed you're supposed to occupy."

Any concern she'd had for Cole evaporated in that moment, frozen underneath his ice.

"No," she said. Just one word. But it went off like a bomb between them.

Cole blinked like she'd just slapped him. "What did you just say?"

"You heard me," she answered.

His jaw clenched, and he took a step back toward her, pointing down at the ground. "After what you did—"

"I didn't do anything!" she nearly screamed at him.

"But you did. *You,* Cole. Not me. All I did was have a perfectly innocent lunch with your brother. You're the one who punched him out over it. You're the one who embarrassed me for no good reason. And now you're the one refusing to explain why you did it, which— since we're talking about contracts—is a violation of the terms you made with me."

She crossed her arms over her chest. "And now you want me to sign a contract and then let you use me to settle whatever grudge match you have going with Max? Nah, man, I don't think so!"

Cole glared at her, his head tipping to the side. "You will sign that addendum, and then you will—"

She glared right back at him, her eyes shining with fury. "You're not going to like what happens if you finish that sentence."

But he took her up on her challenge. "And then you will prove to me you can be trusted."

"Fine!" She threw up her hands, no longer guilty or concerned over what had happened. But just simply disgusted with the whole business. "I'm going back to my own room. Don't come at me again until you're ready to talk to me like I'm a human being."

With that, she turned to leave. "Sunny…" she heard him call after her, his voice ominous and low.

She just flipped him off over her shoulder before walking into her room and slamming the door behind her. She was done taking crap from Cole Benton.

Chapter 20

Cole had messed up. Really, really messed up. He realized that a week later when he woke up to yet another tented sheet.

Of all the cut-throat business deals Cole had ever negotiated, the one he had with Sunny proved to be the most difficult. Not only because she had more business acumen than he'd given her credit for—countering his attack with one of her own for violation of her "talk to me" terms, but also because there was now a supply-and-demand issue.

Cole lifted the cover and inwardly groaned when he saw the straining erection underneath it. Not an unfamiliar sight these days, but damn, if he wasn't sick of dreaming about Sunny all night, and then waking up to the *hard* evidence of those dreams.

Sunny made him furious, Sunny made him feel out

of control. But the fact was, he still wanted Sunny, despite all of this—or maybe because of it? He didn't know, and that made him feel even more out of control. Which he hated.

The pipes creaked in between the wall that separated her suite from his, and soon there came the sound of rushing water.

Cole knocked his head back against the pillow, a whispered cuss word flying out of his mouth. This again. A few days ago, she'd started not only getting up earlier, often around the same time he did for his morning workout, but also taking baths instead of her usual shower.

That meant he not only got to wake up to morning wood, but also imagine her in the smaller guest bathroom. Her naked body, slick with water, as she used one of the penthouse's black washcloths to clean her bountiful breasts…

He threw the sheet off with an aggrieved yank. He'd be damned if he beat himself off again to that image. He was a grown man, he reminded himself when he turned on the shower. The very cold shower. If he didn't have to worry about appearances, he could have any woman he wanted with a snap of his fingers.

But he didn't want any woman, a small voice said in the back of his head. Only Sunny.

And that was the problem.

Sunny wasn't letting him anywhere near her. Seemingly taking a page from his own book of interpersonal dealings, she'd frozen him out, not allowing him to touch her outside of public events. Polite enough when they met up for breakfast every morning, but on the rare occasion they found themselves alone together in a room—nothing but stony silence.

All the late-night visits to his office had come to an abrupt stop. And though he'd been prepared to fulfill his dance class assistant obligation—had even gotten dressed for the class last Sunday—he'd found a note next to coffeemaker from Sunny saying that she'd decided to go in early and wouldn't be needing his help that day.

It shouldn't have bothered him. He had better things to do than lift Lucia and her friends above his head. But it was a good workout—and dammit, he guessed maybe he kind of missed the challenge of learning new dance routines and earning one of Sunny's rare "Good job" comment when he nailed it.

Yes, he'd definitely messed up. He shouldn't have given her that ultimatum, shouldn't have brought sex into it, or let the argument get so ugly. And as Cole drank a pre-workout coffee standing up at the kitchen's granite counter, he had to give it to Sunny. He couldn't remember the last time he'd felt so rotten or unsettled. As punishments went, this one was definitely doing the job.

Cole stopped—thinking about that word *job*. More specifically, what he did when a big client got upset over something that was The Benton's fault. Like when a corporation came in for a national sales meeting to find all their conference rooms already booked up.

"Cole, my boy. A good business is all about keeping the big clients," he remembered his grandfather once telling him. *"If one of them gets upset, apologize with a splashy gift."*

A gift was what he needed. A peace offering to open up new negotiations. A car?

No, too obvious. Sunny would see right through it. He needed something small, but meaningful enough to pack a big punch.

Cole looked around, thinking, thinking...and then his shrewd gaze fell on his state-of-the-art coffee-maker.

Sunny woke up sore and grumpy. She'd danced hard yesterday, choreographing the end of the summer recital, going over each girl's part in the routine again and again until she was too exhausted to think of stupid businessmen and their stupid ultimatums.

But at least the bathtub in the guest bathroom had a jet stream feature. So that morning she poured a small mountain of Epsom salt into the beautiful free-standing tub, just as she'd been doing every morning since she'd started her extreme choreography stint in a fit of desperation to not think about a certain businessman, whose name she wasn't even going to let cross her mind because she wasn't thinking about him. And twenty minutes later, sitting in the bubble bath by herself, with the jets blowing hot water on her sore muscles, she was glad she did.

But one thing continued to get in the way of her complete relaxation. Her muscles were all taken care of, but her core...it was throbbing. Even worse now, because the jets pushing hot streams of water over her breasts and the aching triangle between her legs weren't exactly helping.

Stupid businessman whose name she refused to let herself think. Why did he have to be so good in bed?

Maybe if the sex had been just okay like it had been with Derek, certain parts of her wouldn't be refusing to get on message with the rest of her brain.

She brought her hand down to her swollen sex, probing it with her first two fingers. However, her body's response was less than enthusiastic. Like, "okay, if this all you've got to offer, I'll take it, but it's no C—"

She stopped herself from thinking his name. She hated him now, she reminded herself. She really did. Every time she thought about him sneering down at her, saying he couldn't trust her and demanding she sign a piece of paper like she was some kind of good-time girl who couldn't keep her hands off him or his brother.

The thought of that argument still made her furious a week later. And that should have been enough to cool her down.

Yet it wasn't. Her sex continued to pulse under the assault of the jets, and eventually Sunny gave in, pushing her fingers a little farther down, into her tunnel.

Just a little necessary relief, Sunny told herself, closing her eyes. It was like medicine, in a way, a quick fix that would free her mind, so that she could think of other things like the end of summer dance recital. Not things like the last time her businessman had punished her for being naughty.

She caught her bottom lip with her teeth, moving her fingers faster as she thought about how he'd forced her legs to stay spread wide and butterflied at the knees as he stroked into her. The way he'd hit her clit on the upstroke, getting her closer and closer, even as he intoned, "Don't come yet, Sunny. Not yet..."

"Sunny."

Sunny nearly slipped and fell underneath the water, she was so surprised to hear Cole's voice. Not in her head this time, but in real life. In the very same room as her.

But when she looked up, there he was in the doorway. With the coffeemaker from the kitchen in his arms.

When Cole had walked in with the coffeemaker, it had been meant as a sort of peace offering. But he opened the door to the bathroom without knocking to offer it to her, because he doubted she would have invited him in there if he'd announced his presence first. He'd expected her to be peeved and maybe a little taken aback, neither of which was necessarily a bad thing in a business negotiation

What he hadn't expected was to find her in the bath, teeth on her bottom lip, eyes closed, back arched, so that the top half of her breast were floating above the water, very obviously pleasuring herself.

Cole gave himself a lot of credit for not dropping the coffeemaker.

A lot of credit. Because unlike Sunny he hadn't pleasured himself this morning, and watching her do it was hot as hell. So hot, he wanted to keep on watching, but knew it would be another thing for Sunny to hold against him if she opened her eyes at any point and found him there.

So ignoring how painfully hard he was at the moment, he forced himself to do the right thing.

"Sunny," he called out, letting her know he was there.

She sat up with a gasp, splashing water around and spluttering. And Cole had to work hard to keep a smile off his face as he reached for one of the nearby black hand towels. He passed it to her and she took it, refusing to meet his eyes as he did so.

"I brought you the coffeemaker," he said in the ensuing silence. "You've been spending so much time in the bath lately, I thought you might enjoy having it in here. I can get another one for the kitchen."

He reached over and set it on the ledge beside her before standing back up. Then, since she still had her head turned away from him, refusing to meet his eyes, he let himself drink in the sight of her for a few moments. He'd considered her dark skin beautiful before, but wet and glistening like it was now, he once again had to force himself to do the right thing.

He moved away from the tub. "Anyway, it's a peace offering. I don't want to fight with you anymore, Sunny, and…" He struggled with the words but found he really meant it when he said, "I'm sorry. I'm sorry for the way I acted last week."

The apology was sincere, but Sunny still hadn't turned to look at him. She just sat there, with her knees drawn up to her chest, which made him feel like a pervert, because he couldn't stop ogling her.

He made himself look away. "I'm going to go workout, so you won't have to worry about me coming back in here," he told her, turning to leave. "Feel free to do whatever you want."

He was almost out the door, when he heard her say behind him, "Wait."

He turned around and found her brown eyes on him, frank and curious.

"You were serious last week when you made Tomas drive me to your grandmother's house, weren't you? All that stuff you were saying about control. You weren't joking. You really were trying to punish me for making you lose control at *The Benton Girls Revue*— it wasn't just because your brother was there. It was about control."

It had been for both reasons actually, and Cole wouldn't have been able to tell her where one reason started and the other began, but yes, it had been about control. He silently acknowledged her assessment of the situation with a nod.

"And the things you said to me during that fight, that was about control, too. You were trying to prove you controlled me, right?"

Cole shook his head this time. "Not you. Me. I was trying to prove I could control myself, that you didn't have me wrapped around your finger."

A sad look entered Sunny's eyes then. "I guess I should congratulate you, then, because I think last week proved I definitely don't have you wrapped around my finger. You win."

You win. Two words that he should have felt triumphant to hear from her. But not like this. The look on her face made him feel hollow inside.

"I know I went too far," he told her.

Sunny nodded. "Yeah, you did."

"I know, and I…" Cole took a deep breath, deciding to take a chance. He pulled his workout T-shirt off over his head and pushed down his pants, revealing the shameful fact of his straining erection.

Sunny's eyes widened. "What are you doing?" she asked him carefully.

He came over to stand by the side of the tub. "I'm giving you all the control. Whatever you want me to do right now, I'll do."

Sunny shook her head, baffled amusement entering her eyes. "You're kidding."

Cole shook his own head. "I'm not."

"So if I asked you to take the day off of work and take me somewhere like Lake Tahoe—"

He bent down and tapped the Bluetooth device he'd hooked to the waistband of his workout pants. "Call Agnes," he said, hooking it around his ear.

"Hello, Mr. Benton. What may I do for you?" came Agnes's efficient voice.

"I'm not coming into the office today."

"What— I mean certainly, Mr. Benton, but..." He could hear Agnes's worry through the phone. "You took a half day yesterday, too. Are you okay? Are you sick? Should I send a doctor up?"

Of course he wasn't sick. He rarely got sick and on the few occasions that he had, he'd still come into work. "I'm fine, Agnes—"

Sunny chose that moment to take him in her mouth, her hand encasing his shaft, as she teased her tongue over the mushroom head of his cock. It came as such a shock. Such a pleasurable shock that he expelled all his breath in a quick rush of air.

"Mr. Benton? Mr. Benton?" Agnes said on the other side of the phone. That was when Sunny began really working, bobbing her head up and down as she sucked him in.

It was so unbelievably hot that Cole's basic instinct took over, his hand going to her head to stop her. After last night, he wasn't going to last very long if he let her keep this up. But she knocked his hand away and waggled her finger at him as if to say, "Who's supposed to be in control?"

This was a bad idea. A very bad idea. He realized that as he told Agnes, "I'm fine, but I need to get off the phone. Just clear my day and make a reservation for two at The Benton Tahoe," through a strained voice.

He switched off the Bluetooth without waiting for Agnes's answer, and not a moment too soon. Just a few seconds later, he felt his balls tighten and he unleashed into Sunny's demanding mouth.

Never in his life had he allowed himself to come first. That was a basic tenet of his sex life, but Sunny was smiling as if she'd won some kind of prize. "Oops, it looks like I made you lose all your control and before I could get mine," she said in a sly voice.

She tugged him down, so he was forced to climb into the tub—it was either that are fall.

"I can get back there," Cole vowed, and he went in to kiss Sunny, but she moved her head away from him. "Uh-uh, Cole. You said *I* was in control. That means I get to maul you, not the other way around."

Was that what she thought of his kisses? That he was mauling her? Though, now that he thought of it, he didn't remember a time he'd ever let her kiss him first. He held himself still, waiting to see what she'd do next.

She pushed him backward in the water. "Get yourself ready for me."

Cole didn't understand at first. Surely she didn't want him to please himself while she watched.

Sunny just lifted her eyebrows. "Hey, you caught me doing the dirty solo, let's see what you got."

Cole always recovered quickly with Sunny, but having her eyes on him while he took himself in his own hand, working it up and down, it happened at record speed.

Less than a minute later, and he was able to truthfully say, "I'm ready for you."

Sunny grinned. "Are you sure? Because someone who I never thought would apologize or admit he was wrong, just did. And it's got me all revved up." The water sloshed as she moved across the water toward him. "Are you sure you can handle it? Because it's going to be a long, hard ride."

His cock pulsed at just the thought of Sunny on top of him, her wet breasts dripping with water as she rode him to completion.

But the reality was even better than the dream. She straddled him, biting her lip with a barely suppressed moan as she lowered herself down on his erection. "Oh, *Cole,* so good." She began moving her hips up and down. "Always so good, the way you fill me up. I can't help myself. I've just got to..."

She was incoherent after that, bouncing up and down on his erection with wild abandon. The only thing that kept him from exploding at the sight of her like this, her large wet breasts bouncing as she rode him, was the fact that he refused to disappoint her, to let her regret taking his peace offering.

But no matter how long he held on, it didn't seem to be satisfying her. She ground herself against him, her undulations taking on a desperate tone. "Why can't I... Oh, Cole, I want to so bad, I..."

"Sunny..." he croaked into her ear. He longed to take back control, to give her what she needed to get there. She was becoming unhinged with need, but underneath that, he could sense her exhaustion. However, he had promised.

But then her head fell against his shoulder. "Cole, baby, I can't believe I'm saying this, but take back control. Get me there, baby, please get me there. I'm so close."

Cole didn't need to be asked twice, he grabbed on to her hips, tilted her forward, so that her clit was right where it needed to be when he began moving her up and down on his shaft.

Then he said, "Come for me, Sunny. Come now!"

She came with a scream, clenching him inside her so hard that she took Cole over the edge with her, his entire body seizing up as he involuntarily unleashed a second load.

Eventually Sunny collapsed against him, breathing hard. "I've never— Is it supposed to be like that? So intense? Is that how it always goes down for you?"

"No," Cole answered honestly. "It's never been like that for me with any other woman."

This was a huge statement for Cole, something he wouldn't have been willing to admit, even to himself, a week ago.

And Sunny seemed to sense that. She leaned back and searched his face. For a moment the only sound in the room was the jets pushing water through the tub. Then she stood up and stepped out of the bath.

It occurred to Cole that she was purposefully keeping her back to him as she went to retrieve the towel hanging on the back of the door.

"What would you say now if you hadn't given me control for the day?" she asked him.

"Don't dry off," he answered immediately. "Then I'd tell you to turn around, so I can look at you."

He waited for her to defy him as she so often had in the past, but she didn't.

Her hand dropped in mid-action of bringing the towel to her body and instead she turned around and let him see her in all her glory, completely naked with water dripping down over her large breasts and bare sex.

And that was how Cole ended up getting the top quilt of Sunny's bed wet with bathwater, when he carried her into the guest room and took her again, both of their bodies damp and slippery. It wasn't a decision he could even remember making. One moment he was still in the bath and the next he was thrusting himself into her tight, hot core and releasing an unbelievable third time, shortly after she had.

After that, he went back to bathroom to retrieve the towel she'd dropped, drying her off and then himself, before rearranging her underneath the sheets. He'd expected her to fall asleep right away, but he could feel her eyes watching him as he took the wet quilt off the bed and tossed it outside the door before replacing it with the spare in the closet.

"Are you tucking me in?" she asked him when he brought the new blanket up to her chin.

"You should take a nap before we head out to Tahoe. It's a long drive."

"Yeah, but…" She yawned. "I don't want to sleep without you."

That was when Cole did something else he had

never done. Without another thought, he decided to ditch his workout and take a nap with Sunny.

"I think…I think I might not mind you being in control," Sunny told him when he settled in behind her. From the tone of her voice, she was surprising herself with this confession, too. "I mean, I think I might actually like it. And I might even—you know, need it. I don't know the right term for it."

"Submissive," Cole answered, his voice quiet.

He felt her go stiff in his arms. "I'm not a doormat."

"I know you're not," Cole answered, his voice dry as a desert. If she had been, this arrangement would have gone a lot more smoothly. "Trust me, you've been a challenge from the beginning."

Sunny rolled over to face him, but kept her eyes lowered. "Then why couldn't I get there in the tub without your permission? And you were right about the other day at the show. I was goading you. I think I wanted you to handle me. And the way I keep letting you drag me back here, even when I want to run…"

A hard note crept into Cole's voice. "Look at me, Sunny."

Her eyes raised to meet his and they were filled with a shame that made Cole's heart tighten.

"We don't have to put labels on it," he told her. "I like to be in control and you like for me to take control. This is Vegas. Anything goes. I say we've got a win-win situation here. We win. Not just me. You and me. We win."

She shook her head. "But last week…"

He stopped her right there. "Last week was bad. I went too far. I know that. It won't happen again."

Sunny's eyes went sad again. "I want to believe you, but—"

"Sunny, believe it. I'm not going to risk our arrangement again."

Sunny went quiet, and then she asked. "What did Max mean, when he said he was wondering when the real Cole would show up? Why did he act like you punching him was some kind of victory?"

He didn't want to tell her. Their arrangement was only for a couple more months, long enough for Cole to get Nora kicked off his board. He had no reason to trust Sunny with his deepest secret. No reason at all.

But something in him knew that telling her was necessary for this particular deal. Telling her what she wanted to know was the only way to bring equilibrium back to their relationship.

"You said you had issues the last time we ah... talked. I have issues, too. Or rather I had them growing up," he told her. "After my mother died, I had some problems keeping myself in check, and when somebody pissed me off, said the wrong thing to me— boom. I used to get in a lot of fights. Got kicked out of few schools and went through a battalion of kid headshrinkers. That's the Cole Max knew growing up. Let's just say yesterday wasn't the first time I punched him."

"So are you saying that Max triggered you? On purpose?"

"Maybe. I can't really tell when it comes to him. Max and I got in a few fights when we were younger, but we actually got along a lot better back then," he said. "Caused all kinds of mayhem together. But then my grandfather took me under his wing when I was sixteen, started grooming me to take his place. Things changed."

"Because Max was jealous?"

"Because Max never grew up," he answered. "He's like Peter Pan trying to drag everyone back to Neverland with him. He wants the old Cole back and he's pissed at me for growing up."

"Or maybe he just wants to be close again," Sunny said, her voice soft. "Brothers, like you two used to be. But he's afraid you'll never see him as anything other than a screwup."

Cole stiffened. "Did he say that?"

"No, but that's the sense I got when I had lunch with him," she answered. "You know the only reason I agreed to go was because he promised he'd give me all the dirt on you."

"And what did he tell you?"

"Not one real thing," she answered. "Just a bunch of stories that started with you trying to get him not to do something and him doing it, anyway. He's either really self-absorbed or more loyal than you think, if he didn't tell me about your past."

Cole frowned, thinking about how Max also hadn't let Sunny know that Nora was still in perfect health. Could he really have been reading his brother wrong all this time?

"There's more," he said, deciding then that if he was going tell her anything, he might as well tell her all of it. "My father left my mother for Max's."

"Yeah, I remember you telling me that before," Sunny said. "Is that why you got so angry?"

"No, I got so angry because Max's mother was my

mother's sister. I didn't like the idea of reliving that piece of history with my own brother."

Understanding dawned in Sunny's eyes, and then suddenly it wasn't just him holding her anymore. She wrapped her arms around his neck, and pulled him into a tight hug. "Oh, my gosh, that explains so much. Thank you for telling me. Thank you."

He guessed he must have been more tired than he thought, because he accepted her comforting hug without a fight.

"The point is I've learned the hard way that when I start to get out of control like that, I need to reign myself in," he said into Sunny's shoulder. "I turn off my emotions like a switch until I can trust myself again."

"So that was what happened when we had that argument at my apartment building? When you got hurt and then just stopped," she said, as though she'd finally solved a mystery that had been bothering her for a while.

"Yes," he answered. "But last week I turned my emotions off for a bad reason, because I wanted to punish you, and I didn't trust myself to do it without losing control. The thing is I forgot the second step of rage control. Turn off your emotions and remove yourself from the situation. I didn't remove myself from the situation. I should have waited until I could talk to you without having to flip my emotion switch. But I didn't, and for that, I'm sorry."

For a while, Sunny just hugged him even tighter, as if holding him was somehow helping her process all the information he'd just given her.

But eventually she leaned back and said, "You like to be in control. I kind of like when you're in control.

But it becomes weird if you're *too* in control. So how about this: for the rest of the summer, you can be in control, I'll do whatever you say. But if I want it back for any reason…"

"It's yours," he agreed quickly. "Those are fair business terms."

That must have been the right answer, because she smiled at him, her large eyes full of tenderness, and he smiled back.

As angry as he'd been with his grandmother for putting him in such an untenable position, he couldn't help but feel a little grateful now. His grandmother would get her comeuppance, and he'd get full control of his company, with a Sunny on top—or bottom. Really, Sunny wherever he wanted her. Any way he spun it, this situation with Sunny was going to work out to both of their benefits.

It would all work out just fine.

Chapter 21

This situation with Sunny was not working out, Cole thought to himself after he got off a call with Jasper Whittaker. The Benton Group's oldest board member had been one of the last holdouts on voting his grandmother off the board. He was one of the board's outside directors, which meant he was also outside of Cole's direct sphere of influence, since he was the president of a holding company that didn't do business with The Benton Group. Even more annoying, Cole suspected the widower had a crush on his grandmother, and he refused to even think about voting her off the board. Cole had begun to accept that he might have to move forward without Whittaker's vote, but then he'd remembered his grandfather's rules about holdouts.

"Holdouts are easy, Cole, my boy. All you have to do is whatever it takes to get them to stop holding out."

In Jasper's case, it had taken the detective Cole had hired nearly the whole summer to ferret out a piece of information Cole could use. In this case, a sealed record on his granddaughter for stealing money from Jasper's company when she'd interned there—one her current company, a prominent Las Vegas brokerage firm, probably didn't know about.

"Strange decision to go into money services with her history of embezzling. I know, I for one, wouldn't let anyone with that kind of blemish on her record handle my money."

"It wasn't embezzling. She just had a rebellious streak when she was in college," Jasper answered, sounding irritated but more so worried.

"One that ended in over six figures in losses for your company. Wow, that's quite a rebellious streak. But hey, I believe you, Jasper. I'm just hope this doesn't get out. It could cause her all kinds of problems for her."

Jasper had denied any wrongdoing on his granddaughter's part six ways to Sunday, but in the end, he must have seen the writing on the wall, because he took Cole's offer to help him bury the information—in exchange for a yea vote at the upcoming meeting.

Getting his vote had been more of a principle thing than necessity. The truth was, Cole had the votes he needed to get his grandmother kicked off without Jasper. But when he sprung the vote on his grandmother at Monday's board meeting, he wanted to serve his vengeance cold with a 100 percent vote minus Max.

Jasper Whittaker's capitulation represented a huge victory. By this time next week, The Benton Group would be his to run as he saw fit when he took his rightful position as Chairman of the Board.

Yet the whole time he was on the call with Jasper, some foreign emotion had nagged at him. An emotion he dimly recognized from a very long time ago, as guilt.

And, though the call was supposed to be all about the business at hand, even after he hung up, he couldn't stop himself from thinking about Sunny. What she'd looked like curled up in his bed when he'd left for the gym. How much trust she'd given him over the summer, in the bedroom and out.

How he still hadn't quite figured out how to spin to her what he'd done in order to get Nora off his board. How he hadn't quite come to terms with the fact that she'd be leaving for New York in a few short weeks.

He also thought about the text message she had sent him early that morning.

Can I head out to Palm Springs early to do some shopping? And if so, what do you think I should buy with my own money to wear tonight?

He'd texted her back yes on the condition that Tomas drove her. Then typed out his exact requirements for what she should buy with *his* money, but hadn't gotten a response.

And now hours later, he was more excited about seeing what she'd picked out than he was about his victorious phone call with Jasper Whittaker. He picked up his smartphone and tapped Sunny's name, which had somehow worked its way on to his list of "Favorites" over the course of the summer.

"Hey, Cole," she said, when she answered on the third ring.

"Are you in Palm Springs yet?" he asked.

"Of course I am. I've already finished my shopping, and they were nice enough to let me in the hotel room early—I'm assuming because the reservation's under your name."

Cole grunted. He could almost hear her smiling on the other side of the line when she reminded him. "You said I could go early."

That, he realized, had been a bad decision on his part. If she were still on the premises, he'd tell her to come down to his office for a quickie, if only so he could concentrate on getting the rest of his board meeting speech written up before he left for the weekend.

That was another reason the situation with Sunny wasn't going to his liking. This was the eighth weekend in a row that he'd spent on vacation with her instead of working. And she'd somehow managed to wrangle a promise out of him to spend his next Saturday night starring as what she'd dubbed "the lead lifter" in the community center's summer recital.

True, nothing had fallen to the wayside at work, and nothing other than his dignity would be compromised when he danced with Sunny's girls at their show. It was also true that Agnes had been in a much happier mood lately. He suspected she was using her free weekends to spend more quality time with her husband, and Cole was afraid that if he kept this up too much longer, she'd start expecting to have every weekend off.

Though it wouldn't be that much longer. Sunny

would be moving soon, a voice in the back of his mind reminded him.

"What are you wearing?" Cole asked, not bothering to keep his irritation out of his voice.

"I found a silk romper that sort of looks like the one you destroyed back in July. Seriously, Cole, maybe you should pick a new favorite outfit, one that's not so delicate."

"And underneath it?" he asked.

"My blue lace panties—or was it my black thong?"

"I said no panties in the text message," he reminded her.

"Oh, did you?" Sunny asked. "Then it might be nothing at all. I can't remember for sure."

Cole gritted his teeth against the immediate hard-on that punched out against the fly of his pants. "I don't believe you," he said.

"It's true!" Sunny insisted. "I really don't remember, and the bad thing about this new romper is I'd have to take the entire outfit off to check."

"Sunny…" Cole growled. He'd been right about them not fitting traditional labels with their relationship. In Sunny's and his case, it was less Sub and Dom and more Button Pusher and Button Pushee.

As if to prove his point, Sunny said, "Okay! Okay! If you insist, I'll check." The sound of rustling came from the other end of the call, then, "Oh, that's interesting."

"What?" Cole bit out, his hand opening and closing as he resisted the urge to palm his erection.

"It looks like I forgot to put on a bra when I changed into this outfit," Sunny answered. "Which is weird, because that's so unlike me. Especially, since, oh, my gosh, they've really got the A/C turned up high in here, and my nipples are so hard. Maybe if I massage them a little, they'll go down— Oh, no, actually that only made it worse."

Cole's hand was on his cock now, acting with a mind of its own as he listened to Sunny talk.

She moaned. "I should definitely stop rubbing them. Mmm, it's making it so much worse, Cole, and I can feel myself getting all squirmy down below…" She whimpered. "I'm sorry, Cole, but I'm going to have to pull up my romper and get off the phone without checking to see if I'm wearing panties. If I'm not wearing them, I'm going to ruin this outfit, and it was the last romper they had in stock at the store."

"You can order another one online," Cole bit out.

"Yeah, but that would be a waste of your money," Sunny answered. "Plus, you said you wouldn't be headed out of the office until after six, and I don't want to get in trouble like the last time I touched myself without your permission, so I'm going to have to cut this short. See you when you get here!" she said cheerily.

Before Cole even had a chance to bargain with her to finish taking off the romper while he listened, she hung up.

Cole cursed long and hard.

Then he called her back.

And got her voice mail.

More cursing. Cole punched a few words into his computer thinking about how bad he was going to punish her when he got to Palm Springs five hours from now. Five long hours from now. More if he hit traffic, and considering it was Friday night, that was more than likely.

He called her back again. Straight to voice mail. Then a text message popped up on his screen. Not out of contact, but not answering your calls. For the romper's sake.

He could just imagine Sunny laughing at him while she pranced around his company's luxury suite in the romper, with maybe nothing on underneath it. He'd punish her for that, too, he vowed to himself turning back to the computer.

He typed in a couple more sentences, reminding himself that he had to get his speech for the board done. Sunny almost always used her "control take back" whenever he tried to work while they were spending time together. Nora's big end of summer charity ball was on Sunday, with the board meeting scheduled for first thing Monday morning.

He wasn't going to let Sunny distract him from the last step in his plan, the one he'd been working toward all summer. With determination, he typed a few more words.

Then he punched the intercom button with his index finger. "Agnes?" he started.

"Leaving for Palm Springs early?" she finished.

Cole gritted his teeth. "How did you know?"

"Sunny texted me a few minutes ago that I could make dinner reservations to go out with Greg tonight if I wanted, because I'd definitely be getting off early," Agnes answered with a laugh in her voice.

With a grunt, Cole snatched the jacket off the back of his chair. He was going to make Sunny pay for that one, as well.

Chapter 22

And make Sunny pay he did, as soon as walked in the door. Her poor romper never had a chance, and Sunny gave it a mental apology as it landed irreparably torn less than ten feet from the suite's front entrance.

Cole made Sunny pay for teasing him right there in the outer room, then he made her pay for assuring Agnes she'd be getting off early in the hot tub after they had dinner. Then for the rest of the night, he made her pay and pay again for the ultimate crime of "distracting him from his work."

When she woke up much later the next morning, it was to the feel of his mouth on her now very tender sex, bringing her to completion with long, wet strokes of his tongue over her naked core. He hadn't permitted her to get it rewaxed until a week ago, when he'd gone on an overnight to Los Angeles to talk with one of The Benton Group board members in person.

But now Cole was going at her like a man on a mission, and she came yet again with her fingers threaded through his hair, fully awakened as she arched off the bed. Cole, she decided right then and there, was much better than a morning cup of coffee.

"What was that payback for?" she asked, when he came back up to lie down beside her.

"For looking so beautiful when I woke up," he answered with an affectionate smile.

He'd been smiling at her more and more lately, and it was its own kind of punishment. A total heartstopper that made Sunny feel all goopy inside.

"Kiss me," he commanded.

She did, pulling his tongue into her mouth as she fused her lips over his. She didn't stop until she felt his length harden against her stomach.

"Very good," he said when she finished. He moved against her, and the bottom of his shaft moved against her slit in a way that made her whimper. But then he shook his head. "Not yet. Not until you've had a bath. We went too hard last night to do it again this morning."

What he was saying made total sense.

However, Sunny had obviously stopped prescribing to total sense when she agreed to this arrangement in the first place.

"But I want you now," she whined, her voice low and husky. Then she said a few more things. Button-pushing things that she knew never failed to make Cole lose control and go against his better intentions.

Words that worked every time. Soon he was parting her folds with his long, thick length, pushing in carefully. Too carefully. Sunny had to say some really nasty things to get him moving the way she wanted, hard and rough inside her aching sex, until they exploded at the same time, both lying on their sides, chests pressed together as her core drank in his spasming cock.

"You're definitely not a doormat," Cole said when the orgasm finally let them go, and he pulled out of her.

Sunny knew that. This fling, affair, arrangement—whatever they wanted to call it—had taught her there were ways to give over control without being a doormat. Really fun ways.

She laughed, and sighed with total contentment. "I love you," she thought to herself.

Cole went completely still. "What?"

That was when she realized she might not have only thought that to herself, as she'd promised herself she would when she'd first made the realization that her feelings for Cole extended beyond good sex and pretend dates.

"Nothing," she said quickly and began to move away.

Cole caught her around the waist keeping her there in bed with him. "You think you're in love with me?" he asked her.

Of all the ways she'd been embarrassed in front of Cole, this was easily the worst. "I don't want to talk about it."

"Sunny, I thought the arrangement was clear," he said.

"It is. I'm going to New York. You're staying in Las Vegas. We'll both move on. It's clear."

"But you think you love me."

"I *know* I love you," Sunny answered. "But it's fine, I know where you stand on…feelings. I'm sure I'll get over this love thing when I'm in New York without you right there all the time. It'll take me a few weeks, a couple of months top." *Probably years,* Sunny edited inside her head.

"Sunny…" he began.

"I'd like control back now," she said.

"Sunny…"

"Cole, you promised." She pushed against his chest, desperately wanting to get out of there. "Let me go."

He let her go and Sunny ran into the bathroom, slamming the door behind her.

Cole was beginning to think Sunny might hide in the bathroom forever, but she crept into the outer room fully dressed in yoga pants and a tank top sometime around three. He was seated at the striped couch between her and the front entrance.

She jumped.

"You thought I left?" he asked her.

"I thought maybe you'd gone out. I hadn't heard you moving around for a while."

"Sit down, Sunny," he said.

She hesitated, but came to sit down across from him on the couch.

"So I'm back in control?" he asked her.

She nodded, looking miserable, like this entire conversation was making her unhappy.

"Good," he said. "Then I have another command for you. Stay."

She blinked. "What?"

"Stay in Vegas until this—whatever this is—runs its course."

Sunny blinked her eyes. "You want me to give up my plans? My scholarship?"

"Whatever money they're giving you, I'll double it, and if you want to get a dance degree, you can go to UNLV. I'll pay for it."

He thought these were pretty generous terms, but Sunny looked at him like he'd slapped her. "The University of Nevada Las Vegas doesn't offer a graduate degree in dance. There's no dance program anywhere in Nevada that compares to the one at NYAU. It's the number one program in the nation."

Cole thought about that. "Fine, I'll fly you out every weekend and you'll spend breaks and the summer in Vegas."

Once again, more than generous terms on his part, but Sunny's eyes narrowed. "So your new plan is that we announce our engagement tonight at Nora's ball, and then we what…just keep on acting engaged with me flying back and forth from New York, until when?" She shook her head at him. "Until you get tired of me?"

Cole sighed, not liking at all how Sunny was deciding to take his offer. "I'm not trying to insult you."

"Too late," Sunny answered. "You already have."

Sunny got up from the couch and headed for the door.

"Where are you going?" Cole demanded, following her.

Sunny didn't answer. Just grabbed her purse from where she'd left it on a chair near the front entrance.

"Tomas won't drive you anywhere without my permission."

"It's Palm Springs!" she informed him. "I'm sure I can find a shuttle to take me back."

"What about tomorrow night? The engagement announcement for Nora?" he asked her, furious that she wouldn't even consider his terms, even though she claimed to love him.

Still, he knew it was low to use Nora to manipulate her into turning back around—even for him. Especially since he'd soon have to tell her that Nora was fine, and he'd just been pacifying her until he could make his power move.

Sunny stopped and swung back around to face him. "You're right," she said, her voice even. "I'll come to the party tomorrow. For Nora. But only if you let me go now and don't try to follow me or get in contact with me or evict me or do any of the devious stuff you're always doing to get your way. And you don't have to worry about putting me up in The Benton New York anymore or paying me the money you promised me, because this—" she waved her hands between the two of them "—*whatever it is*—has run its course."

With an angry sadness marring her beautiful face, she turned back around and left, leaving Cole with no choice but to watch her walk away if he ever wanted to see her again.

Chapter 23

It had only taken twenty-four hours to get over having all the hair pulled off one of the most sensitive areas of her body with hot wax. Surely, Cole thought, it should have taken Sunny less time to get over their fight in Palm Springs.

But Sunny had shown up at the entrance outside of The Benton's main ballroom in a light gray ball gown, looking as frosty as an ice princess. Frosty and beautiful.

"Hi," he said, bending down to kiss her on the lips.

Sunny received his kiss, but in a stiff, blank-eyed way. Like she was cardboard cutout of her former self.

"Where did you sleep last night?" he asked her. "I told Agnes to offer you any of the hotel rooms, but she said you'd already made arrangements."

The lease had run out on Sunny's other apartment back in July, so he'd known she hadn't gone back there.

"Jakey's away at a leadership camp, so Pru's couch is free," she answered, no feeling whatsoever in her voice.

"Oh," he said, wondering if this was what it felt like for her when he went cold. "Well, if that couch becomes unavailable, you can come back to The Benton. I want to make sure you have somewhere to stay before you leave for New York."

Sunny didn't answer, just shifted her eyes. "If we're going to do this, we should do this." Then she went into the ballroom, leaving him to follow her in.

Cole couldn't take his eyes off of her after that, even though she'd refused to so much as meet his gaze or say more than a few clipped words to him. Within an hour, he began wishing Nora would get there already, just so Sunny would have to at least pretend to be in love with him, like she claimed to be in Palm Springs.

He thought of that moment with a pang, wishing he hadn't let it catch him so off guard. But he'd been unprepared for the shock of her words, or the way it made him feel. Honored, like having her fall in love with him was the best thing that had ever happened to him, even better than getting named CEO of The Benton Group.

But it wasn't the best thing that had ever happened to him, he reminded himself now, sitting at their table with a barely speaking Sunny. Sunny was a pawn. A beautiful, funny, sexy pawn who he couldn't imagine ever getting sick of as she'd insinuated he would, but a pawn nonetheless. But he didn't want to end up like his grandfather, so besotted that he'd give a woman who knew nothing about business a position of control in his company. Or his heart.

"Trouble in paradise?" Max asked, dropping into the seat on the other side of Sunny at their grandmother's table. "Or did Cole infect you with his stiff shirt disease?" he asked Sunny.

"Hi, Max," Sunny said in a monotone and took another sip of her ice water.

"That's Nora's seat. Your seat's over there," Cole said, pointing to a place card on the other side of the table that he'd shuffled when Sunny wasn't looking, wanting his brother as far away from her as possible.

Max just acted like he hadn't heard Cole. "Hey, Sunny Delight, wanna dance?"

"No, thank you," she answered. "Where's Nora?"

Max shrugged. "Dunno, we got here twenty minutes ago, but you know her. Kept stopping to talk to people in the lobby, including some old dude from the board."

Cole leaned forward to look at Max, alarm sounding warning bells in the back of his mind. "Which board member exactly?"

Max shrugged again. "Hell if I know. All those gray-hairs look alike to me."

Cole was about to press him for more details, when Sunny stood up and said, "Excuse me," and then walked off without a word of explanation.

Cole caught up with her halfway across the ballroom and took her by the hand. "Wherever you're going, I'll go with you," he said.

"Or at least fly me back and forth from there until you get sick of me," Sunny said with a bitter note in her voice.

Her words daggered into Cole and made him angry at himself all over again for not handling her confession of love better. He should have just said thank-you and found a way to bring up extending their arrangement in a way that wouldn't set her off.

Now he realized if he wanted to get back what they'd had before it all blew up in Palm Springs, then he'd have to do something big. Really big.

"Please just let go of my hand," she said, tugging to get it back from him. "We've been acting the part all summer. I think everyone gets it. You don't have to keep on holding my hand everywhere we go at these things."

"No," Cole answered as he walked with her out into the lobby.

"I have to go to the bathroom," Sunny said, pointing to the short hallway off the ballroom's main entrance, where the restrooms were. "Let go."

"No," Cole answered again, not believing her flimsy bathroom excuse for even a second.

"Cole…" She trailed off and expelled a shaking breath, her icy exterior melting. "I can't do this with you. I can't pretend to be in love with you when I'm really in love with you. I can't stand there while you make some fake engagement announcement when you don't feel the way I do. I thought I could, but I can't. Please, I know you wanted to be a robot, but I'm not. I'm a girl with a heart and feelings, and I can't pretend to be with you like that anymore."

"Sunny…"

She shook her head. "You don't really need me here to do this, anyway. Just tell Nora we got engaged in Palm Springs." She held out her hand. "Give me the ring and I'll wear it when I take Nora to *The Benton Girls Revue* this week and I promise I'll act really happy about it. I can do that if you're not there with me."

But she wouldn't be taking Nora to that show this week. Cole couldn't let her. Nora would tell her everything without giving Cole the chance to spin it. He needed more time to figure out how to convince Sunny to agree to his terms.

"Sunny…"

"No, Cole," she whispered fiercely, snatching her hand back. "Those are *my* terms. Take them or leave them, but I can't stay here with you another second."

"Sunny, will you listen to me." He took her by the arms. "I want it to be real."

Sunny shook her head. "What?"

"I want you to agree to marry me. For real. Then I want us to get married. For real, and live together as man and wife. Say yes…please," he added as afterthought.

Sunny's eyes widened with joy. But just for a moment, only one shining moment.

And then everything fell apart.

"Cole!" Nora screeched behind him.

He turned to see his grandmother bearing down on them like a vengeful red-haired harpy.

"You've been going behind my back, trying to get me kicked off the board? Threatening my friends and their family members to get your way like some kind of bully? Why would you ever do that?"

Cole inwardly cursed, knowing without having to be told that Jasper Whittaker had been the board member Nora had been talking to in the lobby. He'd run like a crybaby to his grandmother.

"So that's what you were up to?" Max said, emerging from the shadows, just beyond the ballroom door. "Man, that's cold, bro."

Cole took a moment to glare at his brother. How long had he been lurking there? How much of his conversation with Sunny had he heard?

But he'd have deal with Max later, he decided, and turned back to his grandmother.

"Nora," he said, keeping his voice calm. "We'll talk about this in private." He glanced at Sunny. "Sunny doesn't need to hear this."

"Oh, I think she does, because I set her up with you, thinking she'd keep you from becoming a complete stone. But obviously I didn't realize you were already there. She's the one who needs to be saved from you!"

"Nora, you didn't set me up with her. You threatened to take away my company, the one I'd worked like a beast to grow if I didn't marry her."

Sunny gasped. "What?"

Nora swiped her hand across her body, as if threatening to hand the company he'd built over to his derelict brother had been a minor thing. "I had to figure some way to get you to take me seriously, and tell me, dear, is it my fault the only way to get through to you is to make it about business?"

"Wait a minute," Sunny said, looking between the two of them. "Nora, obviously something has been lost in translation. If Cole's ousting you from the board, it's because he knows it's what's best for you. I know you want to live your last few months on earth fiercely, but it's important that you rest and take care of yourself."

"Sunny..." Cole began.

"What do you mean my last few months on earth?"

Nora asked Sunny. "I'm healthy as a horse. My doctor says I'll outlive all of you."

Max's eyes went wide and he made a little explosion sound behind his teeth. "Well, that secret's *blown*."

Cole's fist bunched up at his side. "Max, I swear if you say another word, I will make sure to break your nose this time. Again."

But Max didn't have to say anything further. From the look in Sunny's eyes, she was already beginning to put it all together. "You're not sick," she said to Nora.

"Of course I'm not sick!" Nora answered.

"But at the *Benton Girls* show you were hobbling."

Nora sniffed. "Okay, dearie, I'll admit to needing a little upkeep these days to maintain this fine figure. But I wasn't going to let a little nip and tuck on the old tum make me miss the show."

Sunny covered her mouth with her hand.

"Sunny, let's go back up to the penthouse," Cole said, feeling desperate and urgent inside. "I'll explain everything in private."

"You told her I was sick?" Nora said to him. "Why?"

"Apparently to get me to pose as his girlfriend while he worked on getting you kicked off the board," Sunny answered, her voice bitter with discovery.

Nora gasped. "You didn't!"

"You left me no choice, *Nora*," Cole roared, turning on his grandmother. "The Benton Group is my life, and I won't have it threatened. Not by you or anyone else. You tried to manipulate me, and now you're going to get exactly what you deserve."

Nora shook her head. "I can't believe you would use poor Sunny like that. *How could you?*"

His grandmother didn't give him a chance to answer before turning to Sunny. "Sunny, I won't let him get away with this. I'll call my lawyer and get the shares transferred before the meeting tomorrow."

Max smirked. "So it looks like I'm going to be the new power player at The Benton Group, after all."

"No, you won't," Nora snapped. "You knew Cole was lying to Sunny, leading her along from the start and you didn't say anything." She patted Sunny on the shoulder. "I'm so sorry, dearie, for everything these worthless boys have put you through. That's why I'm going to give *you* my shares in The Benton Group tonight."

"What?" both Cole and Max said in unison.

"You heard me!" Nora answered, her voice sharp as a knife's blade. "You both need to learn that people aren't pawns to be used in your childish rivalry."

"No," Sunny said. "I won't let you do that, Nora."

"Sunny, maybe you don't understand," Nora said, her eyes full of pity on Sunny's behalf. "Cole doesn't really have feelings for you, after all. He was just using you to get his revenge on me. You don't owe him anything. Nothing at all. Let me do this for you. It's the only way he'll learn."

"No," Sunny said again. Just one word, but its power resonated over them all.

Her eyes landed on Nora. "You were wrong to try to force Cole to marry me."

"Yeah, you were," Max agreed. "I mean you could have at least opened with a date and gone on from there."

Sunny shook her head. "Even a date would have been wrong. Cole is a grown man who has worked extremely hard to make The Benton Group what it is. He has a vision for the company and you can't just ruin everything he's worked to achieve in order to get your way, Nora. That's not fair. Or right."

Nora frowned, having obviously never thought about it that way before. "Maybe that's true," she said with a sniff. "But still, he had no business using you the way he did."

Sunny shook her head. "No, this is my fault. He told me exactly what he was the first day we met, a businessman first and foremost, and I chose not to believe him. Then I did something even more stupid. I fell in love with him."

Max and Nora stared at her, stunned.

But Sunny's eyes landed on Cole. She still wasn't any good at hiding her real emotions, and Cole could see every ounce of hurt and pain his actions had caused her. "Lesson learned."

With that, she turned and walked away.

"Sunny…" He started to go after her, but Max moved to stand in front of him.

"Let her go with some dignity, bro," Max said. "It's the least you could do."

"The very least," Nora agreed, stepping in beside her youngest grandson. "I'll give you my chair position on the board, you don't have to vote me out, but only if you let poor Sunny go in peace. She's right, I was wrong to ever force you on her. I think we can all agree now that you don't deserve her or her forgiveness."

Cole stopped, not because of Nora's offer to give him control of the board, but because of the realization that dropped down on him then like a ton of bricks.

Sunny had been nothing but good to him, forcing him to be a better person, and even defending him against his grandmother despite the humongous wrong he'd done her. Cole realized then that both his brother and his grandmother were right: she deserved her dignity, and Cole didn't deserve anything. Especially not her.

He let her go, watching her dash across the lobby and out The Benton's front doors.

Thanks to Sunny, he'd gotten everything he wanted. But watching her walk out of his life forever, he'd never been more bereft.

Chapter 24

"How did you do it?" Rick demanded as soon as Sunny answered the phone. "You've got to tell me."

"Do what?" Sunny asked, balancing her phone in the crook of her shoulder as she loaded up Pru's small hatchback with the cat tutus for tonight's recital.

It had been money she couldn't afford to spend to get the costumes, but Cole had promised the girls he'd buy them new costumes for the show, and she didn't want to disappoint them.

"Cole Benton's secretary just came by here," Rick told her. "Allison? Andrea?"

"Agnes," Sunny supplied, wishing the name of the woman she'd considered a friend by the end of summer didn't now bring her such pain.

Her mind went back to the last time she'd spoken to Cole's assistant, two days after Nora's ball, when

Agnes had called to coordinate sending Sunny's things over to Pru's apartment.

"I'm not sure why you broke up, but it's obvious he cares about you," Agnes said in a moment of unprofessional candor. "I mean, he took off work. *A lot!*" she said in the same tone of voice others would use to talk about someone taking an unexpected trip to the moon.

Sunny had cut her off right there, telling Agnes she didn't need or want any of the clothes she'd kept over at Cole's. In fact, she'd insisted, "feel free to burn them."

"What happened? I wish either you or Mr. Benton would tell me. Is there anything I can do to help?" Agnes asked, her voice distraught.

Sunny had just smiled sadly. As amazing an assistant as Agnes was, even she couldn't fix this.

"Okay, then how about this matter of the apartment at The Benton New York. Mr. Benton was adamant about me giving it to you. He says you can stay there as long as you want."

Sunny had been forced to get a little more firm then, telling Agnes she wouldn't be using the apartment, and that as much as she liked Agnes, she didn't want her to call her anymore.

"I need a clean break from Vegas," Sunny explained. "And everyone that reminds me of…Vegas."

Though they both known when Sunny said *Vegas,* she meant *Cole.*

Known and understood. Agnes had solemnly gotten off the phone with a promise not to bother her again.

But Rick was on the phone now, bringing up Agnes's name.

"Yeah, Agnes. She came down here this morning with my new contract. Gave me a twenty-year extension. Said I could die with the show if I wanted, because it wasn't going anywhere."

"That's great, Rick!" Sunny said. "But I had nothing to do with it. Mr. Benton and I aren't seeing each other anymore."

"Uh-oh, what'd he do? Must've been big, cuz obviously The Third's trying to get you back. I say let him have you. Maybe I'll get a big raise."

"That's not going to happen," Sunny answered.

"We'll see. He's spending an awful lot of money on 'never going to happen.'"

Sunny sighed. Rick had no idea. In Cole's messed up mind, he probably thought of keeping *The Revue* open as honoring his part of the original agreement. It had nothing to do with her, really. Just another piece of business for him.

I want you to agree to marry me. For real. Then I want us to get married. For real, and live together as man and wife.

The memory of his marriage proposal cracked her heart open all over again. Why had he done that? To keep her from leaving before the jig was up? To keep her as his sexual plaything? Of all the things he'd done, pretending he'd really wanted to marry her had been the thing that haunted Sunny the worst.

God, she'd be happy when she finally stopped thinking about him every other minute, when her body stopped aching, because he hadn't touched it in so long. When she stopped waking up every morning, only to get hit with a fresh wave of sadness because Pru's couch wasn't his bed.

How stupid could she be? First she'd let herself get

tricked into Cole's power play on Nora, and now she couldn't get herself to stop longing for him.

"Rick, I'm really happy to hear the news. But I've got to go or I'm going to be late to the recital," she said, settling into the front seat of Pru's car.

"So I guess that means there's no chance of you coming back to the show?"

Sunny's heart sunk, but she guessed this was the perfect opportunity to finally tell him. "Actually, I'm moving to New York next week…"

After a summer of avoiding this conversation with Rick, it turned out not to be as bad as she'd thought it would. Rick was disappointed that he wouldn't be seeing her in person for a couple of years, but he wished her luck and told her that if she ever moved back to Vegas to look him up. He'd use his dance contacts to make sure she landed someplace good doing whatever she wanted.

"You're a great kid, Sunny," he told her. "You deserve to get everything you want in life."

It was a truly touching thing for Rick to say, and was completely ruined when Cole Benton's image immediately sprang into her mind on the echo of "everything you want." She was beginning to think of Cole's memory like a lethal snake. Always lingering in dark places, lying low, and then striking her with its sharp teeth just when she least expected it.

Sunny cursed herself. Then she cursed again when she noticed the time on her car clock. Thanks to her heart-to-heart with Rick, she was now officially late.

She hung up with Rick and drove like a madwoman over to the community center.

Carrying the large box that was so unwieldy, she

had to position it in front of her in a way that meant she couldn't see past it, but that was okay. The class was using their small dance studio as their dress room, since the community center's auditorium didn't have a real one, and she knew how to get there by heart.

"Here are your tutus, girls," she said, coming into the studio box first. "Find your size and put it on quick like a bunny. We need to go over the routine a few more times before we hit the stage. I had to make a few changes to the choreography."

"Why'd you change it up," she heard Lucia demand as she walked the oversize box over to the bench where the girls sat down to take off their street shoes.

"Because Cole's not going to be here to do the lifts, and I'm not strong enough to take his place. So we're going to have to figure out how to do those parts without him." She set the box down and began sorting out the sizes, slapping the fur-lined tutu outfits onto the bench in piles.

"Why can't Cole do it?"

"I just told you he's not going to be here, now can you just get into your costume, Lucia? Please!" Sunny snapped, feeling as if the child's questions had pushed her to the end of her rope.

"But we're already in our costumes," Lucia whined behind her, "And Cole's right here!

What? Sunny's back went ramrod straight and she turned around to see the little girls not only all dressed up in the cat costumes she'd picked out for them, but Cole...in a hooded fluffy dog costume with long droopy ears. Like the girls, his nose was painted black, but unlike the girls his eyes weren't filled with happiness, they were filled with pain. As if seeing her for the first time since Nora's ball was breaking his heart in two.

Or maybe she was only imagining that was what it was, since that's exactly what it did to her to see him standing there.

She shook her head. "No, Cole. Don't do this."

"Sunny," he said, his voice ravaged. "Please hear me out. Please listen to me."

The sixteen girls' heads ping-ponged back and forth between them like they were at a tennis match.

"No, I don't know why you're here, but go away. Please just go away."

"No, I tried do it your way, and if you feel anywhere near as bad as I have over the last week, then it's not working," he said, his voice hardening. "I'm not going to go, not until you hear what I have to say."

"Ooh, this is better than a telenovela," Lucia observed, and got a few nods of agreement from her fellow dancers.

"Why are you doing this to me?" Sunny demanded, her heart beating as if it were set to shatter inside her chest any second now. "This has been one of the most terrible weeks of my life. Why would you come here? You're only making it worse."

"Oohhhh!" the girls said, their heads moving back to Cole for his response.

"Because I love you," Cole shouted back at her. "Dammit, Sunny, I love you. I was an idiot not to realize that sooner, but trust me, just going a week without you made it clear. I can't work, I barely sleep. All I can do is think about you and how stupid I was for letting you get away, for lying to you in order to become Chairman of the Board. Because guess what? I've got the chairmanship. Nora signed the paperwork earlier in the week. So I finally got everything I wanted, but it doesn't mean jack, because you aren't there to share it with me."

The girls couldn't have possibly understood what half of that meant, but they all said, "Awwww!" just the same, as if it were the most romantic thing they'd ever heard.

But not Sunny. She shook her head at Cole. "What's your endgame this time, Cole? You're telling me you love me, why? To get back at Max? To prove something to Nora? What is it this time?"

Cole shook his head. "My only endgame is you, Sunny. You're all I want. That's why I'm going to have to renege on my offer to put you up in The Benton New York."

Sunny was about to tell him what she'd told Agnes, that she didn't want the apartment, anyway, that she'd figure it out on her own before she ever accepted another thing from Cole Benton, but he didn't give her a chance to speak.

"You can't stay in my hotel, Sunny. Not without me."

"What?" she said, her anger giving way to confusion.

"Sunny, I want to move to New York with you. I don't have to be here to run The Benton Group. I can work out of New York. It'll make things a little more difficult, but I don't care. I just want to be with you, Sunny. If you want you can even have the chairmanship of The Benton Group. I'll give it to you like my grandfather gave it to my grandmother. I'll do anything. Just—Sunny, please…"

Her eyes widened as Cole went down on his knees and pulled a ring box from out of the pocket of his dog costume. "Sunny, please…"

The rest of his words were drowned out by the girls screaming their heads off when he opened the box to reveal a ring with a diamond so big it looked like costume jewelry.

Sunny stood there frozen to the spot, unable to process what Cole was doing. What he'd promised. What he was asking her to promise.

"Dios Mio! Dios Mio! Dios Mio!" Lucia screamed, as if this really was the end of a telenovela. "Say yes, Miss Sunny. Please say yes!"

Epilogue

She'd said yes. Cole was still having a hard time believing it, even as he watched Sunny getting dragged up to The Benton's ballroom floor by Pru a few months later. A Beyoncé song played overhead and a crowd of showgirls and young old-money heiresses gathered to see who would catch Sunny's bouquet, now that she was officially taken.

"You're probably feeling like one smug bastard right now," Max said, appearing beside him.

Cole thought of the vacation he and Sunny had planned. Two months in a little bungalow on a small island in Tahiti during her winter break from NYUA. All that time alone together before they had to return to New York—he'd probably be able to come up with some very creative punishments for his bride in the their back and forth game of control.

"One *lucky* bastard," he corrected Max.

"Yeah, well, you're just lucky she didn't take you seriously about becoming the Chairman of the Board…" Max rubbed the bump on his nose, the only thing that kept him from a girlish level of prettiness. "She's a saint for taking you back. And she's hot as hell, too? Yeah, you definitely got lucky, bro."

Cole's eyes narrowed. His brother's observations about his wife's looks weren't a thing he cared to hear. "Don't make me regret making you my best man, Max."

Max shrugged. "You only did it because Sunny made you. She gave me that whole speech about this being the first step in mending our relationship, too." He pointed his finger toward his mouth and pretended to gag on it.

"Speaking of relationships, I've decided our gran might not have been so wrong about the benefits of marriage, after all. You have a year."

Max scrunched his forehead. "A year for what?"

"To settle down and get married," Cole answered. "Otherwise, I'm cutting you off. No more salary for doing absolutely nothing, and I'll exercise Gran's option to buy your shares in the company at their original value. So you'll only get what they were worth when Grandpa died, before I took over."

Max stared at him, then he burst out laughing. "Okay, you got me, bro. That was a good one. I didn't even know you were capable of making jokes. Sunny's really changed you."

Cole grinned back. It was true. Ever since he'd made the temporary move to New York to be with Sunny, he'd been smiling and laughing more than he ever had before. He was even occasionally known to make a joke.

Max's face lit up. "Hey, your hottie wife's hottie bridesmaid just caught the bouquet. What's her name again?"

"Prudence," Cole answered. "But everyone calls her Pru."

"Yeah, Pru," Max said with a wink. "Better go congratulate her."

Max handed him his glass of champagne and went off to make his move on Pru. And he must have been right about Sunny having really changed Cole. The old Cole would have made sure Max knew he wasn't joking, that he really was going to cut Max off if he didn't get his act together and show he could commit to something. But the new Cole decided to wait to tell him until tomorrow morning at the wedding breakfast, because hey, it was his wedding day.

"You're smiling," Sunny observed a few minutes later when she rejoined him at the main table. "Wonder what's going through your mind?"

"How lucky I am," he answered truthfully.

Sunny chuckled and whispered in his ear, "I don't know about that. You told me to get a lace gown, and I got this silk sheath instead. Oops! Now I'll definitely have to be punished on our wedding night."

Cole smile grew even bigger, thinking of Sunny lying across his bed, begging him all night to do with her exactly as he pleased, and made a mental edit on an old Vegas standard.

Luck would definitely be a Sunny tonight.

* * * * *

The first two
stories in the
Love in the Limelight
series, where four
unstoppable women
find fame, fortune
and ultimately…
true love.

LOVE IN THE LIMELIGHT

New York Times
bestselling author
BRENDA JACKSON
&
A.C. ARTHUR

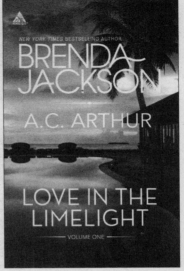

In *Star of His Heart*, Ethan Chambers is Hollywood's most eligible
bachelor. But when he meets his costar Rachel Wellesley, he suddenly
finds himself thinking twice about staying single.

In *Sing Your Pleasure*, Charlene Quinn has just landed a major
contract with L.A.'s hottest record label, working with none other than
Akil Hutton. Despite his gruff attitude, she finds herself powerfully
attracted to the driven music producer.

Available now wherever books are sold!

HARLEQUIN®
™ www.Harlequin.com

KPLIM11631014R

The last two
stories in the
Love in the Limelight
series, where four
unstoppable women
find fame, fortune and
ultimately…true love

LOVE IN THE LIMELIGHT
—— VOLUME TWO ——

ANN CHRISTOPHER
&
ADRIANNE BYRD

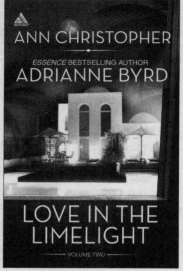

ANN CHRISTOPHER
ESSENCE BESTSELLING AUTHOR
ADRIANNE BYRD

LOVE IN THE
LIMELIGHT
—— VOLUME TWO ——

In *Seduced on the Red Carpet*, supermodel Livia Blake is living a glamorous life…but when she meets sexy single father Hunter Chambers, she is tempted with desire and a life that she has never known.

In *Lovers Premiere*, Sofia Wellesley must cope as Limelight Entertainment prepares to merge with their biggest rival. Which means dealing with her worst enemy, Ram Jordan. So why is her traitorous heart clamoring for the man she hates most in the world?

Available November 2014 wherever books are sold!

HARLEQUIN®
™ www.Harlequin.com

KPLIM21641114

REQUEST YOUR FREE BOOKS!

2 FREE NOVELS PLUS 2 FREE GIFTS!

KIMANI™
ROMANCE

Love's ultimate destination!

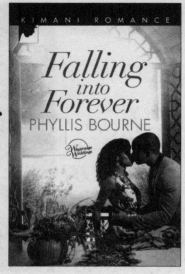